"Don't you apologize again," Barrett warned Della when she opened her mouth. But he winced and waved that off. **"I haven't worked it all out in my head yet, but then I figure neither have you."**

He was right about that. "The only thing I'm certain of right now is that I want this baby, and I need to keep him or her safe."

"Him or her," he repeated, and judging from his expression, those pronouns made it very real to him. A boy or a girl. Their son or their daughter. "Yeah, I want the baby safe, too, and that's why we have to declare a truce. For now, let's take our past relationship off the table and concentrate on finding a killer."

That sounded, well, good. "Is it doable? I mean, us declaring a truce?" Della asked.

The corner of his mouth lifted in that half smile.

HER CHILD TO PROTECT

USA TODAY Bestselling Author

DELORES FOSSEN

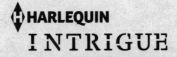

HARLEQUIN

INTRIGUE

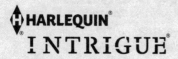

Recycling programs
for this product may
not exist in your area.

ISBN-13: 978-1-335-28462-4

Her Child to Protect

Harlequin Enterprises ULC
22 Adelaide St. West, 40th Floor
Toronto, Ontario M5H 4E3, Canada
www.Harlequin.com

Printed in U.S.A.

Delores Fossen, a *USA TODAY* bestselling author, has written over one hundred novels, with millions of copies of her books in print worldwide. She's received a Booksellers' Best Award and an RT Reviewers' Choice Best Book Award. She was also a finalist for a prestigious RITA® Award. You can contact the author through her website at www.deloresfossen.com.

Visit the Author Profile page at Harlequin.com.

CAST OF CHARACTERS

Sheriff Barrett Logan—This cowboy cop is thrown into a dangerous murder investigation where his mother is the main suspect and his former lover could be the killer's next target.

Deputy Della Howell—Even though Barrett is her ex, she still has deep feelings for him. She's also keeping a secret that could destroy their already fragile relationship.

Robert Casto—An unscrupulous rancher whose murder spurs an investigation that puts several people, including Barrett and Della, in grave danger.

Alice Logan—Barrett's estranged mother. She wants to repair the relationship with her son, but first she has to prove that she didn't murder her lover, Robert Casto.

Wilbur Curran—A wealthy cattleman whose dirty business dealings could be the reason Casto was killed. He could also be behind the attempts to murder Barrett and Della.

Lorraine Witt—Robert Casto's former lover, she might do anything to avenge his death, but the real killer could be setting her up to look guilty.

Rory Silva—His sister's murder could be tied to the current investigation, and it's possible that Rory knows more than he's saying.

Chapter One

Sheriff Barrett Logan aimed his flashlight in the ditch and looked for a dead man.

There were no signs of him, but then Barrett hadn't believed there would be. That was the problem with getting an anonymous tip. It could be a hoax. However, since he was the sheriff of Mercy Ridge, Texas, checking out hoaxes was part of his job description.

Especially this one, which had come in the text he'd gotten from an unknown number.

There's blood near the county marker. She finally did it. She murdered him.

Barrett didn't know who this *she* was, but that wasn't the only word that had stood out for him. *Blood*, *finally* and *murdered* had also grabbed his attention. If this was indeed some kind of prank, then the person who'd sent the text had clearly wanted to embellish the details in such a way to make him jump right in and investigate.

Keeping watch around him, Barrett moved away from his truck that he'd left parked on the road. He'd put on his emergency flashers and kept on his high beams in case someone was out this time of night. Not likely, though. This was a rural road with a mile or more separating the sprawling ranches that dotted the area. Plus, it was nearly one in the morning, and most folks had long gone to bed. Mercy Ridge wasn't exactly a hotbed of partying and such.

Barrett fanned the flashlight over the sign that the texter had mentioned. The sign wasn't just to let drivers know they were entering another county but also to mark the lines of jurisdiction. Barrett and his deputies policed this side, but if the supposed body was beyond the sign, then that would fall under the jurisdiction of the Culver Crossing PD.

The cool spring rain spat at him, soaking the back of his shirt and his jeans. Thankfully, though, his Stetson was keeping the water out of his eyes, making it easier for him to see a long stretch of the ditch. Definitely no body and no blood in there, but he did see something else.

Footprints, maybe.

Someone or something had trampled down the weeds on the other side of the ditch. Weeds that practically arrowed toward a thick cluster of trees and underbrush.

Avoiding the trampled down parts, Barrett jumped across the ditch, his boots sinking into the wet ground, and he adjusted his flashlight again. However, before he could follow the trail, he heard the sound of an approaching vehicle. One that braked to a screeching stop right behind his truck. It was a Culver Crossing cruiser, and Barrett started muttering some profanity before the deputy stepped out.

Della Howell.

She was definitely someone he hadn't wanted to see tonight. Or any other night for that matter. The last time they'd spoken nearly two months ago, she had made it crystal clear that she hadn't wanted to see him, either. Yet, here she was.

Barrett hadn't expected her to have changed much in these two months, and she hadn't. Well, except for that troubled look she was giving him. Then again, Della often looked troubled, and there was often plenty of wariness in her crystal blue eyes.

The rain had already gotten to her, he noticed. There were strands of her shoulder-length dark brown hair clinging to the sides of her face and neck. Her shirt was doing some clinging, too. Definitely something he hadn't wanted to notice.

Della pulled in her breath and released it

slowly, the kind of thing someone would do when steeling themselves up. It didn't seem to help, though, because at the end of it, there wasn't much change in her expression.

"Did you get a text telling you that a body was out here?" she asked.

Her voice and expression were as cool as the night rain, and it reminded Barrett that it hadn't always been that way. Of course, the noncool times had happened when she'd been in his bed. Since that was another reminder he didn't want or need, he pushed the thought aside.

"Yeah," he verified, and purposely turned back to his search.

He tried to look unruffled by all of this, but his thoughts were going a mile a minute. Why had someone texted both of them? Was this some kind of sick ploy to get them back together? If so, heads were going to roll. Of course, he couldn't actually come up with anyone who'd want that. Certainly not his brothers, because they knew he was still stinging from having Della put an end to their *relationship*.

As Barrett had done, Della fanned her flashlight over the ditch and surrounding area, and she stopped on the trampled down weeds. She hopped over the ditch, moving right behind Barrett. Too close to him, but then she was likely trying not to disturb the area that had alerted both of them.

"If an animal did that, it would have to be a big one," Della muttered.

Yep, but there were some bears in this area, or it could have been deer. However, it didn't seem like that, and an uneasy feeling settled in Barrett's gut. Since he'd been a lawman for over a decade, he'd learned not to dismiss that feeling, and that's why he rested his right hand over his sidearm.

With Della right on his heels, Barrett continued walking, moving slowly along beside the trail that something or someone had left. He still couldn't pick out actual tracks or footprints, but then the rain could have washed them away.

And then something caught his eye.

Barrett kept the flashlight on the object for a few seconds, making sure he was seeing what he thought he was. It was a woman's purse.

Della obviously saw it, too, because she stepped around him, going closer. She stooped down to examine it, and even though she didn't ask any questions, Barrett could practically feel them going through her mind.

Who did this belong to, and how'd it get here?

The cream-colored leather handbag was lying on its side and was wet with rain, but it wasn't damaged. Nor did it look as if it'd been there for a while. In fact, it looked as if someone had dropped it there very recently.

"It's open," Della said, angling her head so that she could see the contents. "There's a wallet."

Good. Because once they knew the owner, they could figure out how it got here. And why.

Della looked up at him, his flashlight spotlighting her expression. It was a mix of dread and Texas-size concern. "I recognize it." She swallowed hard. "It belongs to your mother."

That took Barrett's uneasy feeling to a full gut punch. Hell. This wasn't going to be good. He hadn't seen or spoken to his mother in years, and to the best of his knowledge, she didn't stray this close to Mercy Ridge.

"No," Della said, as if reading his mind. "Alice wouldn't have come here."

And Della would know that about her. Unlike Barrett and his brothers, Della was close to Alice. Or rather she had been when Della and he had still been together. He figured that hadn't changed because, unlike him, there wasn't bad blood between Della and his mother.

Bad blood.

It was an expression that people threw around a lot when it came to estrangement, family feuds and such, but it was deeply personal for Barrett. Even after all this time—over two decades—

he could still see his father lying on the floor of his office. Could still feel the vicious punch of grief and the instant realization that nothing would ever be the same again.

And his mother had been the one who'd caused that.

"Alice wouldn't have had a reason to come here," Della added.

Barrett welcomed the sound of her voice. It drew him back to the only place his thoughts should be right now and that was figuring out what had gone on here. Bad blood, old memories and an attraction for Della shouldn't be playing into this.

"No, but someone could have stolen the purse and ditched it here," he argued.

It was the most logical theory he could come up with, but it still didn't make sense. If someone wanted to toss away a stolen purse, there were a heck of a lot of easier ways to do it. Just throwing it into the ditch would be faster than coming into these woods.

Barrett glanced around them again, looking for any signs of the person who might have left the purse. Nothing. No sounds, either. Just the steady rain and the pulsing of his own heartbeat in his ears.

Della slipped a thin plastic glove from the back pocket of her jeans, and once she had it on, she looked at the wallet. When she had it open, Barrett had no trouble seeing his mother's driver's license.

Muttering some profanity, Della put the wallet back in the purse and took out her phone. Of course, his mother's number was there in her contacts. Had been for as long as Barrett could remember. It had been one of the many sticking points between Della and him when they'd been together.

Even though Della didn't put the call on speaker, Barrett had no trouble hearing it go straight to voice mail, and he got a jolt of memories when he heard the recording of his mother's voice. Bad memories. As he'd done with his body's reaction to Della, he pushed that aside.

"I'll text Jace and ask him to go out to Alice's house ASAP to check on her," Della said as she did just that.

Jace was Della's boss, Jace Castillo, the sheriff of Culver Crossing. Since that was also where Alice lived and Jace and Alice were friends, it was a logical request. But the *ASAP* also let Barrett know that Della was plenty worried. So was Barrett. Just because he didn't care much for the woman who'd given birth to him, it didn't mean he wouldn't do his job. If something had happened to her, he wanted to find out.

"Jace will head over to Alice's place now," Della relayed when she got a response from him.

Good, but Barrett didn't intend to just wait around. He turned his flashlight to the ground around the purse. The weeds and grass had been trampled here, too, and that continued, the trail leading deeper into the darkness and toward that thick clump of oaks.

He started walking again but then stopped when he heard a sound. Maybe a moan, and it was coming from that area by the trees. Della must have heard it, too, because she hurried after him when he picked up the pace of his steps. And despite the rain and darkness, Barrett spotted her.

The woman lying in a heap on the ground.

It was his mother, all right.

That got both Della and him moving faster. It also got Barrett glancing around to see if anyone else was there. He wasn't sure what they were dealing with, and he didn't want to be ambushed.

As far as he knew, he didn't have anyone gunning for him, but as a lawman, that was always a possibility. Some people just stayed riled to the core even when they'd gotten what they deserved, and someone could have used this to lure him out here.

His mother was lying on her side, her legs

drawn up into a fetal position, and her arms and hands were pressed over her chest like a shield. She made another moan, the sound of pain, and that's when Barrett saw the gash on her forehead. It was still bleeding, but the rain was washing it away.

Other than that wound, he didn't see any more injuries. However, she was soaked to the bone, her yellow dress clinging to her.

"Alice," Della called out on a rise of breath, hurrying to her. She didn't try to pick Alice up but did lift an eyelid, causing his mother to moan in pain again.

"I'll get an ambulance," Barrett said, making the call.

He estimated that it would take the EMTs about fifteen minutes to get there, and during that time he hoped he'd have answers as to what had happened to her. Hoped, too, that he could tamp down the worst-case scenarios going through his head.

God, his mother looked so weak. And hurt. While Barrett wanted to be immune to the feelings that caused inside him, he wasn't.

"Why are you out here?" Barrett asked her. His lawman's tone came through loud and clear, and it caused his mother to open her eyes again. She looked in his direction, her gaze spearing his.

"Barrett," Alice muttered. Her voice was watery and weak, just like the rest of her.

"Why are you here?" he repeated, his snap earning him narrowed eyes from Della.

His mother shook her head, groaning at the movement, and she glanced around as if seeing her surroundings for the first time. "I don't know."

Hell. That wasn't the answer he wanted, and he moved in closer to get a whiff of her breath. No scent of alcohol, but her eyes looked a little glazed. He'd never heard rumors of his mother being a drug user, but maybe that's what was going on. Of course, that still didn't explain squat.

"You think she was in a car accident?" Della asked him.

Maybe. But there'd been no other vehicles on the road, and Barrett was pretty sure he would have seen a car that'd crashed into a tree or a pasture fence.

"Oh, God." Della practically gasped that out, and it definitely got Barrett's attention. However, it took him a moment to realize why Della had said it.

The blood.

She had eased back his mother's arms, no doubt to see if there were any other injuries, and there apparently were. The front of her dress had blood on it, and probably because of the way she'd been holding her hands, the rain hadn't washed it away.

Della kept her movements gentle, but she continued to move Alice's arms and leaned in to examine her. When Della looked back up at him, there was a whole new wave of concern in her eyes.

"Her dress isn't cut," Della said, her voice shaky now. "I don't think it's her blood."

Barrett cursed before he could stop himself, and the words from the text came back to him. *There's blood near the county marker.* Yeah, there was. What the person who'd sent that text hadn't mentioned was that it was on his mother.

But why?

How?

Getting those answers was a high priority. So was the ambulance. Once it arrived, then he could collect Alice's clothes and have them processed at the lab. For now, though, maybe the woman herself could give them some info.

"Think hard. Did someone bring you out here?" Barrett asked.

Alice just gave him a blank look. Not Della, though. Barrett thought there was a different kind of alarm on her face.

"Did, uh, Robert have anything to do with this?" Della whispered to his mother.

Barrett didn't ask who this Robert was. He knew it was likely Robert Casto, a rich rancher from Culver Crossing. Along with having a reputation for being a heavy-handed jerk, Robert was also his mother's lover. Or rather he had been last Barrett had heard, but then he didn't keep his ear to the ground for gossip about Alice.

"Robert," Alice repeated, but she didn't add any more to that. Her eyelids fluttered back down.

"Keep questioning her," Barrett told Della, and he took off his hat to hand it to her. "And hold this over the blood." The rain was already washing away enough of it, and he wanted to preserve the scene—even if he didn't know exactly what this *scene* was.

"Where are you going?" Della asked when he started to step away.

"I want to have a look around," he mumbled, and then added, "Keep watch."

That brusque order had likely offended Della. After all, she was a cop just as he was, but at the moment she was a distracted one. A woman she considered a friend was wounded, in a place she shouldn't be, and she had blood on her.

Yeah, they needed to keep watch.

In the distance Barrett heard the sirens. They'd made good time, but he still had a couple of minutes before the EMTs would arrive on scene and reach his mother. Della would no doubt take care of that, too, and could guide them to their position by using her flashlight.

Barrett used his own flashlight to look at the ground beyond the trees. There were more trampled weeds, and the sight of them put a harder twist to the knot in his gut. What the hell had gone on here? He'd assumed his mother had come here from the road, but maybe she'd come through the woods. But that didn't make sense, either. The nearest house was a good mile away, and there was no trail or back road that led from Culver Crossing to here.

Behind him, he could hear Della continue to ask his mother questions. Could hear the sirens getting closer, too. But Barrett kept moving, kept fanning the light over the rain-soaked ground.

And then he saw it.

Another person. A man this time, and like Alice, he was lying on the ground in a crumpled heap. He was beneath a thick oak and was on his side, his face turned down so that Barrett couldn't tell who it was.

Barrett didn't run to him. His lawman's training kicked in, and he approached from the side so as not to disturb the trail that led directly to him. There could be prints or trace on that trail, things that he might need later when this turned to a full scale investigation. There was no *if* about that. There would be an investigation.

The man was wearing dark pants, cowboy boots and a white shirt. Or rather some of it was still white. The thick oak had done a decent job of sheltering him like an umbrella, and because of that, Barrett could see what was all over the man's clothes.

Blood. And lots of it.

Barrett could also see the gleaming silver handle of the knife that someone had plunged into the man's chest.

Chapter Two

Della wanted to go after Barrett, but she had to take care of a few things first. Alice was her top priority. The woman was too pale, and every inch of her was shaking now. She was injured and in shock. And the scene had to be preserved, too.

Even if any potential evidence didn't lead in a good direction.

Mercy, why had Alice been attacked? And who or what was at the end of the trail that Barrett was following?

"Don't move," Della told Alice, and despite the woman's moaning protests, Della hurried away from her to the ambulance that had just stopped behind Barrett's and her vehicles. The driver angled the ambulance so that the headlights were illuminating the ditch and grassy area where Della waited for them.

Two EMTs quickly got out, and Della didn't bother asking their names. However, she did identify herself, tapped the badge clipped to the waist of her jeans, and she motioned for them to follow her.

"Walk here so you don't disturb the scene," she said, pointing to the makeshift path that Barrett and she had created.

Della ran back toward Alice and was glad that the EMTs did the same. "The victim is Alice Logan, age fifty-seven. She has a head injury," she explained, and judging from the sounds they made, they recognized the name.

Of course, they did. The EMTs were from Mercy Ridge, and everyone there knew Barrett and his brothers. Everyone knew the scandal that Alice had created, too. It didn't matter that the scandal had happened a long time ago because gossip about that and the aftermath would go on forever.

And Della should know.

She had personal knowledge of family tragedies.

When they reached Alice, the EMTs rushed to her and immediately started to examine the woman. While they did that, she went after Barrett, trudging through the underbrush that scraped her boots and jeans. He wasn't hard to find since he had stopped only about twenty feet away, and he had his flashlight aimed at something.

No, at *someone*.

With her attention frozen to the man on the ground, Della automatically slowed her steps until she reached Barrett's side.

"I've already called this in," he told her. Unlike her, he was firing glances all around, and that's when she noticed he'd drawn his gun.

Della did the same, her service weapon sliding against the leather when she pulled it from her shoulder holster. Just the fact that she needed to take such measures sent her heart rate soaring even higher than it already was. Whoever had done this to Alice and this new victim could still be out there. Ready to attack her and Barrett, too.

"He's dead?" Della asked, already knowing the answer. He certainly wasn't moving, and even though she could only see the side of the man's face, it wasn't the skin color of the living. Plus, the knife appeared to be right in his heart.

"He's dead," Barrett verified. Then, he paused. "That's Robert Casto."

Sweet heaven. That jolted through her like a lightning bolt, and Della frantically shook her head, hoping that it wasn't true. But all it took was a closer look for her to verify it. And the verification caused her to realize that things had just taken a very bad turn for Alice.

"I arrested Casto just yesterday for assaulting

your mother," Della blurted out, and she turned
to Barrett to see if he'd known that. Judging
from the profanity he growled out, he hadn't.
"He made bail right away," she added.

That had surprised no one, including Della.
Casto had plenty of money. Plenty of attitude,
too, making Della wonder why Alice had ever
gotten involved with him in the first place. A
shrink would probably say that Alice wanted to
punish herself, and if so, Casto was a surefire
way to do that.

"Did Casto put that cut on her head?" Barrett asked.

"Maybe. But if so, she didn't have it yesterday when I arrested him. According to her statement, they'd gotten into an argument. Then, he'd
grabbed her by the hair, slapped her and tried to
stop her from getting in her car to leave. Alice
managed to get away from him, and she came
straight to the police station. She was pretty
shaken up, but the only visible injury she had
then was a red mark on her left cheek."

The moment Della mentally repeated what
she'd just said, the words in the text came back
to her.

She finally did it. She murdered him.

Had the person who'd sent that message been
talking about Alice? Mercy, she hoped not.

"Alice didn't do this," Della insisted. But she

figured Barrett wouldn't believe her. And he didn't.

"Try to stay objective," Barrett said, and it was a warning. One that stung because she knew he was right. Being impartial was part of being a good cop, but it was impossible to override what she knew in her gut.

"Alice didn't return blows when Casto hit her," Della quickly added. She was careful not to say *your mom*. That would be like poking a stick at a coiled rattlesnake. "She was scared but not hotheaded and stupid." Della stopped, reconsidered. "Unless this is a case of self-defense."

Della could see that playing out. Maybe Casto had kidnapped her, brought her here, and Alice had gotten away. They could have fought, and in order to save her life, Alice might have stabbed him.

"You said they'd argued yesterday," Barrett reminded her. "About what?"

This certainly wasn't going to make Barrett believe Alice was innocent, but Della couldn't withhold evidence. She had to believe that when all the pieces of this were put together, the facts would clear Alice.

Even if at the moment, it didn't look as if that would happen.

"Alice wanted to end the relationship," Della

said. "Casto apparently didn't care much for that and got physical with her. He had a history of that. Not with women, not that I know about anyway, but he's punched several of his ranch hands."

Barrett didn't question her about that, but she figured he'd want more details later. Right now, he was likely doing the same thing she was, trying to piece this together. If Casto had a history of violence, then it could have come back to bite him.

Or rather kill him.

Della stooped down to get a better look at the body so she could see if there was anything to back up her theory. There was so much blood. Casto's shirt was covered with it, and it was dripping off the fabric and seeping into the ground. The flashlight made it look as if it were on display. And it slung Della right back to another place, another time.

Another violent death.

Her best friend and fellow deputy this time. Francine Silva. Francine's killer had also used a knife. It had left a pool of blood. Lifeless eyes. A senseless death, and her killer hadn't been caught, hadn't been punished.

Somehow, that was the hardest part to take.

Francine had been murdered by an unknown assailant. An intruder who'd broken into her house and killed her when she'd surprised him. Or rather that was the theory. Ironic that even though Francine had been a deputy and had lived her life surrounded by cops, her murder was still unsolved.

Sometimes, the deepest cuts came from not knowing who'd done it. And from not having been able to stop it.

Della shook her head, pinched her eyes shut a moment and tried to will away the images. It'd been over a year since she'd had a panic attack, and she didn't want to have one now. She was a cop, she reminded herself. Armed and trained. And she needed to do her job. If she didn't, then heaven knew what would happen to Alice. Despite Barrett's warning about her staying objective, she doubted he'd do the same when it came to his mother.

"Are you okay?" Barrett asked.

Della groaned softly because she heard something in his voice that she didn't want to be there. Sympathy. She saw it in his dark eyes, too, when she stood and met his gaze head-on.

A shared sympathy had first brought them together. That and the attraction. Cold, dark pasts colliding with a bright scorching heat. It had been the right mix for them to share a bed on a regular basis. Not enough, though, for them to get beyond, well, themselves and the baggage caused by their pasts.

Now that he didn't have on his cowboy hat, the rain covered his thick black hair and his face. A warrior face, she'd always thought. Tough and angled. Hot. Yes, Barrett had gotten a darn good deal out of his gene pool when it came to his looks.

Barrett's gaze stayed locked with hers, maybe trying to decide if she'd told him the truth about being okay. She wasn't, of course. It wasn't just the blood and the fear for Alice, but Della had to deal with something else.

She felt a tug of the old attraction.

Thankfully, it quickly cooled, though only because of the footsteps she heard coming their way. They both pivoted in the direction of the sound, and she soon spotted a familiar face, making his way toward them.

Barrett's brother Daniel, who was also a Mercy Ridge deputy.

Since Daniel was keeping on the same path Barrett and she had taken to get to Casto's body, he'd no doubt seen his mother.

Daniel gave Della a nod that was neither friendly nor hostile, and he went to stand by his brother. The family resemblance was strong, not just in their faces but also their tall rangy bodies, and Daniel's stance showed their united front.

Alice wouldn't be getting any warm fuzzy hugs from either of them. Heck, neither would Della. Barrett might not have spilled the details of their breakup to his brothers, but they wouldn't need to know the facts to be on his side. They'd always be on Barrett's side.

"Any idea what happened here?" Daniel asked Barrett.

"Not yet. But the dead guy is Robert Casto."

Daniel swore under his breath, shook his head. "She killed him?" He hitched his thumb over his shoulder in the direction of their mother.

"No," Della said.

At the same moment Barrett answered, "That's to be determined." Barrett tossed her a scowl and took out his phone. "Someone texted both Della and me this about thirty minutes ago." He showed Daniel the message that she had already memorized.

There's blood near the county marker. She finally did it. She murdered him.

"She," Daniel repeated, and Della had no doubts that the deputy believed that it referred to his mother.

"Yeah," Barrett verified as if he'd read his

brother's mind. "You were just with Alice?" he asked, and Daniel nodded. "Did she say anything useful?"

Daniel shook his head. "She's unconscious at the moment. The ambulance is about to take her to the hospital. I figured as soon as the doctor checks her out, you'd question her."

"I will," Barrett confirmed.

"I want to be there for that," Della insisted, causing both Daniel and Barrett to look at her.

The two didn't exactly give her glares, but it was close enough. Della might get the real-deal glares, though, when she insisted that Alice not be questioned until she had her lawyer present.

"The medical examiner is on the way," Daniel explained several moments later. "I can wait here for him and start processing the scene." He glanced around and tipped his head toward Alice. "I believe she's on Mercy Ridge land, but it'll be close. Not so sure about the dead guy, though. I think the boundaries for Culver Crossing start right about where he is."

Sweet heaven. What a mess if that was true.

Daniel's attention settled on Della again. "Will your *boss* give us a hassle about who'll have jurisdiction on this?" he asked.

He said *boss* in the same tone as discussing a bad cold. There was no love lost between Jace and him, and again it went back to Alice. The

Logan brothers wouldn't want Jace on their turf, but Della seriously doubted that Jace would just stay away—even if it turned out that this wasn't in Culver Crossing's jurisdiction. Of course, Barrett likely thought if Jace and she got control of the investigation, they would look the other way at anything wrong Alice might have done.

"Sheriff Castillo will give us a hassle," Barrett concluded before Della could figure out how to answer that. "But call a reserve deputy to help you figure out who'll be primary on this case. Or if we'll have to share the investigation."

Della winced at the idea of sharing. Jace and Barrett could hardly be in the same airspace without snarling at each other, and it wouldn't help that Jace would also be trying to protect Alice. Both Jace and Barrett were good cops, and they would do their jobs, but adding Alice to the mix would fire tempers on both sides.

And Della would be caught in the middle.

Della tried to push that aside, and she followed Barrett when he made his way back to the ambulance. The EMTs already had Alice loaded in the back.

"Restrain her until we know what we're dealing with," Barrett called out to them.

"Restraints?" Della protested. "Is that necessary?"

"It is if Alice is a killer. Or even a suspected

one—which she is. Right now, she's the prime suspect in her estranged lover's murder, because I'm pretty sure Robert Casto didn't commit suicide."

Of course, Della had known that, but it felt like another gut punch to hear it. *Alice was a murder suspect.*

Barrett motioned for the EMTs to head out. He started toward his truck, no doubt to follow the ambulance, but he stopped and looked at her.

"I should probably not waste my breath, but there's no reason for you to come to the hospital right away," he said. "It'll likely take the doctor a while to examine her, and that'll give you enough time to go home and change into dry clothes."

Della wasn't sure if he was genuinely concerned about her or if it was his attempt to keep her out of this. Either way, it wouldn't work.

"I'll be fine," she assured him, hoping she sounded a lot stronger than she suddenly felt.

"Suit yourself," he grumbled a split second before he got in his truck and drove away.

Della got in her cruiser, but she didn't follow him. Not right away. She started the engine and took a moment to gather her breath. Then, another moment to try to tamp down everything inside her that she was feeling.

Oh, mercy. Why was this happening now?

The timing couldn't have been worse. Barrett and she were already at odds. Odds that she had decided she was going to have to mend. She couldn't see a way around that.

For now, though, mending would have to wait. But soon, very soon, Barrett was going to need to know the truth.

That she was pregnant with his child.

Chapter Three

"Hell," Barrett grumbled under his breath, and he thought that one word described this mess.

He had a dead body, an injured suspect who happened to be his mother, a looming juris-diction dispute. And Della. No way to forget her since she'd been right on his heels when he arrived at the hospital. She'd stayed on his heels, too, as Barrett had gone to the ER, where Alice had already been carried into an exam-ining room.

Hell was definitely the right word.

Della's breakup with him was still too fresh for him to completely put away his feelings, but he had to try so he could focus on what could turn into a nasty tangled investigation. Still, it was impossible not to remember that she'd ended things so she could get on with her life.

Yeah, her exact words.

Get on with my life.

Translation: Della wanted the whole shebang.

Marriage and kids. Barrett could have possibly given her the first, *possibly*, but not the second. Considering he'd had to practically raise his younger brothers, he was about as far from being daddy material as one could get.

Barrett went to the examination room and tapped. With Della looking on, a nurse opened the door. He knew her, of course. Gina Corona. She was scowling, probably because she didn't appreciate the interruption, but when she saw that it was Barrett, her expression softened.

"I need her to stay restrained," Barrett told Gina. "And I have to Mirandize her."

No softening of her expression that time. Gina sucked in a hard breath. "I see." She gave an uneasy glance over her shoulder. So did Barrett, and he saw the doctor, Lyle Tipton, already starting his exam. "She's not conscious right now."

Barrett nodded. "As soon as she's awake, come out and get me. I don't want her saying anything until I've read her her rights."

Gina gave a shaky nod and shut the door. And speaking of *shaky*, that applied to Della, as well. She didn't challenge him, though, on the restraints or the instructions he'd just given Gina. Della just stepped away from the door and him.

Since he was going to need as many allies as he could get on this investigation, he took out his phone to call his other brother, Deputy Leo Logan. Along with the county CSI team, Daniel would take care of supervising the processing of the crime scene. The ME would deal with Casto's body, but there was other legwork to be done, and he could rely on Leo for that.

"I heard about the murder," Leo said the moment he answered. "Just got off the phone with Daniel. What do you need me to do?"

"Plenty." Barrett dragged in a long breath that he figured he was going to need, and he moved even farther away from Della.

Since the ER waiting room wasn't that big, she'd likely still be able to hear him, but by turning away from her, he wouldn't have to see that stark look on her face. A look that conveyed she was no doubt worried about his mother.

The one good thing about this was there was no one else in the waiting room, so prying eyes and ears wouldn't get any juicy gossip fodder. But since someone could come walking in at any second, Barrett decided to spell this out fast to Leo.

"There was no vehicle anywhere near the crime scene," Barrett explained. "I need you to call out every reserve deputy we've got to go through the area and find out how Alice and Robert Casto got out there. Concentrate on the back roads and ranch trails. I also need you to try to trace a text I got. I'm sending it to you now. Yeah, I know it's a long shot," he added after he'd forwarded the message to his brother.

"I'm on it." Leo paused a heartbeat. "Anything else?"

"Daniel will request it, but you push, too, to get the results as fast as you can. I want to know if there are prints on the knife that killed Casto."

"Got it." Leo paused. "You really think Alice murdered him?"

Barrett glanced at Della to see if she'd heard that, but if so, she didn't have a reaction to it. She was sitting in one of the chairs, the heel of her right palm pressed to her forehead. Her eyes were closed, and her breath was coming out in short gusts. She looked sick or something, and he decided it was probably the *or something*. Seeing all that blood had probably triggered some flashbacks for her. It certainly had triggered some for him.

"I don't know if Alice killed him," Barrett answered honestly. He knew Alice was capable of doing some cruel things. Things that cut to the core. But murder.... He just didn't know.

"What about notifying Casto's next of kin?" Leo continued. "You want me on that?"

"I'll have Daniel do that after the ME confirms the ID." Of course, they all knew the dead guy was Robert Casto since both Della and he had done a visual identification, but Barrett wanted to go by the book on this one.

"Do you even know who his next of kin is?" Leo pressed.

"Don't have a clue. I just wasn't interested in Alice's latest bedmate." And yep, there was bitterness in his voice. Barrett had long given up trying to remedy that.

"Are you okay?" Leo asked a moment later.

Barrett figured he'd be getting that question from his grandfather, Ben, and anyone else who knew that this would eat away at him. "I'll focus on the job," he assured his brother. The badge had always grounded him, and Barrett was heavily counting on that happening now.

He ended his call with Leo and glanced around, looking and listening for anyone who could give him answers as to Alice's condition. Nobody was there except for Della. If he didn't get an update soon, he'd go back into the examining room to see what was going on.

"There was so much blood," Della muttered, and judging from the way her eyes flew open, she hadn't intended to say that aloud.

If they'd still been lovers, or even friends, Barrett would have pulled her into his arms and tried to comfort her. But since she'd been the one to put an end to their relationship, there wasn't much chance he could provide any comfort now. However, it punched at him some to see her like this.

"Yeah," Barrett said, sinking down in the chair next to her.

Both of them had certainly seen their share of spilled blood. Della on the night a man had murdered her best friend, Francine. Barrett, on the clear spring day when Alice had walked out on her husband and her sons so that she could run to another man's bed. Barrett hadn't known all of that, though, before he'd gone into his father's office at their family ranch and found him lying dead on the floor. A self-inflicted gunshot wound to the head.

There was no way for Barrett to turn off the image of his father. No way to erase the emotions.

No.

Since that day when he'd been only twelve years old, it was always with him. And while it was the reason he'd become a cop, it was also why he saw and felt the past every time he thought of Alice. His so-called mother might not have pulled the trigger for his father, but she had certainly put the tragic events of that day into motion.

"You're the only person I know who's as messed up as I am," Della said. The burst of air that left her mouth was a little like a hollow laugh.

Barrett made a sound of agreement and hoped that would be enough to stop her from saying more. It didn't.

"At least I was an adult when I found Francine," Della went on. "You were just a kid when your dad died."

He had been indeed, and Barrett knew that had added an extra layer of grief. Grief that sometimes felt so thick he was surprised others couldn't see it coming off him in waves. Still, he'd survived and had been damn lucky that his father's dad, Ben, had stepped up to take in Barrett and his brothers. If not, they might have been forced to go with Alice, to live with the woman they blamed for their father's death.

Of course, Barrett didn't blame only Alice. No, she shared that "honor" with the man she'd run to when she'd left her husband and her kids.

Jace's widowed father, Brett Castillo.

Alice had not only run to her lover, Brett, she'd also moved in with the man and Jace. Had mothered Jace when she hadn't bothered with her own kids. Even after Brett had died in a car accident just a few years later, Alice had stayed in Culver Crossing.

"I go over Francine's file at least once a week," Della went on. "I look at every clue, every photo. I think of all the things that I could have done to make sure her murder didn't happen."

Hindsight could be downright mean, and it wouldn't do any good to tell Della that there was nothing she could have done to stop Francine from dying. That's because Barrett, too, knew all the details of the case since he'd pored over it with Della. In fact, that's how they first landed in bed.

Almost two years ago, shortly after Francine's death, Della had come to him as a friend and fellow cop. First, to have him go over the investigation with a fresh eye. Then, she'd poured out her pain and misery to him, cried on his shoulder, and they'd ended up becoming lovers. Barrett had never been under any illusions that it was more than friendship and comfort between them, but sometimes he wondered if they hadn't both been so *broken* if things would have been different.

The sound of footsteps yanked Barrett out of that miserable mental trip down memory lane, and he immediately got to his feet. But it wasn't a doctor or anyone else on the hospital staff. It was Sheriff Jace Castillo. Tall and imposing, Jace glanced around the room as if he owned it—at least that was Barrett's take—and he went straight to Della when he spotted her.

Jace didn't ask her if she was okay, but he put his hand on Della's shoulder and gave it a gentle squeeze. However, there was no trace of gentleness when the lawman shifted his gaze to Barrett.

"You've already questioned your mother?" Jace asked, and again it was Barrett's take that he emphasized those last two words.

"Not yet, but I will as soon as the doctor clears her." Barrett made sure he emphasized the "I." He didn't want to go into that examination room and have three cops trying to question Alice. Or worse—one doing the questioning and two treating her with kid gloves.

Jace volleyed some glances between Della and him as if he was trying to decide how to handle this. Barrett decided to clarify things for him.

"Alice was found in Mercy Ridge," Barrett explained. "The dead guy likely was, too, but just in case he wasn't, the prime suspect was taken into custody when she was in my jurisdiction. Even if this turns out to be a joint investigation, I want the suspect's statement on record."

"So do I," Jace assured him. "I'm not looking to cut corners. In fact, I have some of my deputies out scouring the area, and I've instructed them to stay on the Culver Crossing side."

There was a smart-ass edge to Jace's tone. One that Barrett didn't have time to respond to because the door to the examination room finally opened, and Gina gave Barrett the come-forward motion with her hand. Della immediately got to her feet, no doubt to follow him.

Barrett ground out some mumbled profanity. "You can watch and listen, but she talks to me first."

Jace obviously took that as an invitation because he went with Della. However, they stopped in the doorway. Maybe because of the warning glare that Barrett shot them.

Dr. Tipton stepped to the side, adding some notes to a medical chart, and Barrett went closer to the examining table. Lying on her side, Alice was awake, but her eyes looked filmy and unfocused. She had fresh stitches on her forehead. No restraints, though. Something that didn't please Barrett. But at least Alice didn't seem ready to try to bolt right out of there.

"Barrett," Alice murmured, her voice much the same as when he'd found her on the ground. "Thank you for being here."

He nearly tapped his badge to remind her that his being here wasn't by choice, but instead he turned to Gina. "I want her clothes bagged," Barrett instructed the nurse. Then, he looked down at Alice's hands. No signs of injury, and there didn't appear to be anything under her fingernails, but he'd have them checked to make sure.

Dr. Tipton looked up from his notes, his gaze sliding to Della and Jace before he shifted his attention to Barrett. "It's okay if they're here?"

"For now," Barrett grumbled.

The doctor nodded. "Mrs. Logan has a concussion and some contusions on her right side and buttocks."

Barrett had to get past the sucker punch of hearing Alice being called Mrs. Logan. As far as he was concerned, she'd given up the right to use that surname twenty-three years ago. Still, it was legally hers.

"She also has a lump on the back of her head," the doctor went on. "It didn't need stitches, but it appears someone hit her. Or maybe she got it in a fall."

In other words, it clarified nothing.

"She said she hadn't been sexually assaulted," Dr. Tipton added a moment later.

"I wasn't," Alice verified, and her voice was a hoarse whisper. She cleared her throat and repeated it, this time loud enough for all of them to hear.

Behind him, he heard Della's breath of relief. The idea of sexual assault had occurred to Barrett. Hell, lots of things had occurred to him, but first and foremost was that Alice had rammed that knife into Casto's chest.

"The EMTs restrained me," Alice went on. "They must have thought I did something wrong."

So, Alice didn't know about Casto. Or rather she was pretending not to know.

"I didn't do anything wrong," the woman insisted, looking past Barrett and at Della and Jace.

Alice's allies.

Barrett held up his hand to stop Alice from saying anything else so he could Mirandize her. As he said each word of it, she looked even more unsteady, and Barrett could practically feel Jace's glare drilling holes in his back.

"Do you understand your rights?" Barrett asked Alice when he was finished.

Alice nodded. "But I don't need a lawyer. I just want to tell you what happened so we can clear all of this up."

Barrett doubted that it would be that simple. "How'd you get out in the woods tonight?"

Alice opened her mouth, closed it. For someone who wanted to spout her story, she sure took her time getting started. "I don't know," she finally said. "I don't remember."

Barrett managed not to groan, but even a

woman in a partially dazed state had to see the frustration and skepticism on his face. "Exactly what do you remember, then?" he pressed.

Again, she took her time, moistening her lips first. "I was in my garage, getting out of my car, and I heard a rustling sound behind me. Before I could turn around and see who it was, I got hit on the head." She touched her fingers to the spot and moaned softly. "He hit me again right as I fell. This time on my forehead."

"He?" Barrett immediately questioned.

"I believe it was a man, but I didn't get a good look at him because the light was out in my garage."

Barrett would check that out to see if someone had tampered with it and if there were any signs of struggle.

"What happened then?" Barrett continued.

Alice shook her head and winced a little. "I don't remember anything else until I woke up outside. It was dark and raining and someone was dragging me through the grass."

"Who was dragging you?" Barrett asked, knowing he was going to get another head shake from her. And he did. "Was it Robert Casto?"

Alice hesitated as if considering that. "No." Her gaze darted away from him, and Barrett didn't know if that's because she was lying or just embarrassed that she'd been involved with someone like that.

Someone who was now dead.

"The man was bigger than Robert," Alice went on. "A lot bigger, and he was wearing black pants and shirt. And boots," she added as if just remembering that. "Not cowboy boots but the steel toed ones that lace up."

"But you didn't see his face?" Barrett pressed.

Alice stayed quiet a moment. "Just glimpses. I didn't recognize him. I don't know who he was."

Maybe. Barrett still wasn't buying this. He shifted his position, leaning in so he could see Alice's expression when he asked her the next question. "Did you kill Robert Casto?"

There hadn't been much color in Alice's face, but what little there was drained completely. "Robert..." She shook her head. "He's dead?"

Well, if she was faking surprise, she was doing a darn good job. In fact, her reaction went past mere surprise to shock.

"He's dead," Barrett verified, his voice flat. "Someone killed him. Was it you who did that?"

"No. God, no." The words rushed out of her mouth, and Alice pushed herself up to a sitting position. Not easily. She was clearly still wobbly. "Robert's dead," she muttered, lifting her trembling hand to the doorway.

Barrett wasn't sure who Alice was reaching

for, but it was Della who came forward, and she took hold of Alice's hand. "It'll be okay," Della whispered, and it sounded like a promise.

One that Barrett knew Della couldn't keep.

If Alice had lied and had been responsible for Casto's death, she would pay. And Barrett would have to be the one to make sure that happened.

Jace stepped closer, too, sending Alice a sympathetic look, but he moved back to the doorway when his phone rang. Barrett ignored him and kept his attention on Della and Alice. It was possible that Alice might say something to her friend that she wouldn't say to the son she'd abandoned.

"Robert's really dead?" Alice asked. Her eyes filled with tears.

"I'm sorry. It's true." Della paused. "Alice, he was murdered. Someone stabbed him."

Alice sucked in a hard breath, her hand flying to her mouth, and those tears didn't stay in her eyes. They spilled down her colorless cheeks.

"I can't hug you," Della murmured when Alice reached out to her. "The lab will need to process your clothes."

Barrett saw it then. Even though he'd Mirandized Alice, it was obviously just now sinking in that she was a murder suspect or at least she'd come in very close contact with the killer. He wasn't legally required to spell that out for her just yet unless he actually arrested her, but he would have told her exactly that if Jace hadn't spoken first.

"I need a word with you," Jace told Barrett.

Barrett felt the annoyance from the interruption slide through him, but he went to the doorway while keeping an eye on Della and Alice. If Alice said anything else, he wanted to hear it.

"That was Glenn Spence, one of my deputies, on the phone," Jace explained. "He was searching the old ranch trails near the crime scene and he found an SUV parked there."

That got Barrett's full attention. "Does it belong to Casto or Alice?"

"Neither. It's a rental, and it appears to be on the Mercy Ridge side of the woods." A muscle flickered in Jace's jaw. "There was a guy inside. No ID on him, but he was dressed all in black and was wearing black steel toed boots."

"I want to talk to him," Barrett insisted.

Jace shook his head. "You can't. He's dead."

Chapter Four

Dead.

That was not what Della had wanted to hear. Right now, they needed answers to keep Alice out of hot water, and this boot-wearing man might have been able to provide them with that. But at least they had his body and his vehicle. Once they knew who he was, they could go from there, and maybe fill in some of those much needed answers.

"I'll head out to the dead man's SUV," Barrett said before Della could volunteer to do just that. It was a reminder that the location of the vehicle was in his jurisdiction. "If Alice says anything else, I want to know about it," he added to Jace, and it sounded like a warning.

"I want to go with you," Della insisted.

Barrett had already started walking, but that stopped him, and when he turned toward her, she saw the debate in his eyes. A long debate that lasted several snail-crawling moments before he finally nodded. Maybe he thought her going with him was the lesser of two evils and that at least this way, she wouldn't be at the hospital with his mother.

Jace gave her a look, too. One that she didn't have any trouble interpreting. If she learned anything, he wanted her to tell him. And she would. Jace and she might not be able to stay 100 percent objective when it came to Alice, but both of them wanted the woman's name cleared ASAP.

When Barrett and she stepped out of the hospital, Della noticed the rain had finally stopped. That could be a break because it meant there was a higher chance of having the crime scene preserved. Daniel was dealing with that, and he was a good cop. If there was anything to find, he would find it.

"Coming with me isn't necessary," Barrett grumbled as they headed toward his truck. Like Della, he glanced around, looking for any signs of trouble.

"That depends. This way you don't have to deal with Jace."

Though it did occur to her that Barrett might have as much trouble or more dealing with her. Still, it would give them a chance to talk, and while she wasn't looking forward to that, she did want to feel him out. To see how Barrett might handle the baby bombshell she would soon have to tell him. Her guess was that he wouldn't handle it well, but she didn't have a choice about telling him. He had to know.

God help her.

Some movement to their left had Barrett and then Della pivoting in that direction, and she saw a man getting into a car. A man she instantly recognized. She slid her hand over her weapon just as Barrett did the same.

"Wilbur Curran," Barrett said under his breath, and he added some profanity. "What the hell is he doing here?"

Della was wondering the same thing, and the question didn't have her relaxing her hand on her gun. Curran was a wealthy cattleman, and there were rumors that he hadn't used legal means to come by all his wealth. She'd already had too many raw memories tonight, and seeing Curran only added to them. It was no doubt the same for Barrett, since at one time Barrett had been trying to tie Curran to Francine's murder.

"Curran's guilty of something," Barrett muttered. "I just don't know specifically what."

Della considered that while she got into Barrett's truck. "Are you still investigating him?"

"Yeah." Barrett didn't hesitate with his answer, and that loosened some of the pressure Della was feeling in her chest. Despite her having ended their relationship, Barrett hadn't stopped seeking justice for her friend.

Of course, Della hadn't stopped, either. She was convinced that something Francine had been investigating had gotten her killed. But what exactly? Della still didn't know, but Francine had been looking into a money laundering scheme that was linked to Curran. No proof of that link, though. No proof of anything, really, and that's why Curran wasn't behind bars.

Barrett pulled out of the parking slot, but he slowed to a crawl when they passed Curran. The man looked at them, his gaze spearing them, and what she saw was plenty of arrogance and cockiness. In other words, his usual reaction.

"Two days ago I requested a search warrant for Curran's financials," Barrett said, getting Della's complete attention. "His connection to money laundering just keeps gnawing away at me. So does the possibility of him having had something to do with Francine's death. I didn't get the warrant," he quickly added, "but I'm going to keep trying."

"Does Curran know that?" she asked.

"You bet. And that's why he's glaring at me right now." He paused. "And you're thinking he might have had something to do with what happened tonight. I'm not ruling it out, but for now I'm sticking with the obvious. Casto and

Alice were at odds, and now Casto's dead. No need for me to try to connect Curran to this."

No, but Della would look into it.

"Thank you," she said.

Barrett's gaze connected with hers for a few seconds before he turned back to the road. Or rather the road and the rearview mirror. He was glancing behind them, no doubt checking to see if Curran was following him. He didn't seem to be.

"What are you thanking me for?" Barrett asked.

"For not giving up on Francine."

His huff let her know that she'd just insulted him. She hadn't intended to do that, but it just felt as if with each passing day people forgot a good cop had been murdered. Della had no intention of forgetting it, and she was glad for all the help she could get in finding Francine's killer. And Barrett's attempts to help her hope-fully meant that he wasn't holding their breakup against her.

Or at least his feelings about that had mel-lowed.

Della very much needed him to mellow so she could tell him what he had to hear. That in about seven months, he'd be a father.

Since she'd seen the plus sign on the preg-nancy test, she'd been trying to figure out how to tell him, and she hadn't come up with a single scenario where she could see him being happy about this. Not once had Barrett ever mentioned his desire for children.

In fact, just the opposite.

His bitter childhood had left him not trusting relationships, not wanting a deep connection to anything that could tear him apart again. He loved his brothers, she was certain of that, but Della suspected he held back his feelings even with them. She didn't suspect, *she knew* that he'd done the same with her.

Barrett had had no problem keeping their relationship at just sex, and he'd reminded her countless times that he wasn't capable of more than that. That's why her baby news was going to shake him to the core.

"I noticed earlier that you were too pale," Barrett said out of the blue.

That certainly pulled her out of her thoughts, and Della hoped that no one else had picked up on that. She didn't want anyone guessing about the pregnancy until she'd told Barrett.

"Are you sick, or has all of this just gotten to you?" Barrett pressed as he drove out of the town and back onto the country road.

There it was. The opening she needed. But the timing was beyond bad. After all, they were heading to a crime scene, their second of the night, and this one had a dead body that could hopefully give them answers as to why Casto had been murdered and Alice attacked. Still, maybe timing was always going to be "beyond bad" when it came to Barrett and her.

Della pulled in a long breath that she was certain she would need, but before she could even get out a word, she spotted the vehicle just ahead. Not driving or parked on the side of the road but rather right in the middle of it.

Barrett obviously saw it, too, because he hit the brakes, his tires squealing and going into a slide on the rain-slick road. He managed to come to a stop just a few yards away from the black SUV.

Because of the dark tint on the windshield, Della didn't see anyone inside the vehicle, but the passenger's side window was lowered a couple of inches.

"Maybe the driver stalled," Della muttered, but she instantly got a bad feeling in the pit of her stomach.

Apparently, Barrett got a buzz, too, because he drew his weapon. Della reached to do the same, but it was already too late. She saw the hand snake out from the window, and she spotted the gun.

Just as the bullet slammed into their windshield.

THE PELLETS OF safety glass flew at him, and Barrett automatically caught onto Della and pulled her lower onto the seat. His first thought was that he wished they were in a cruiser, where the glass and sides of the vehicle would be bullet resistant. But they weren't. They were in his truck, and the shots wouldn't have any trouble getting through to them.

"Did you see who fired the shot?" Della asked, her voice hoarse and shaky. Despite the shakiness, she had already drawn her weapon and was levering herself up. No doubt to return fire.

But the shots stopped her.

Four more rounds came crashing into what was left of the front windshield, and Della and Barrett could do little more than stay down or risk being hit. They were both cops. Both knew they could face possible danger. However, it caused his adrenaline to soar to know that Della could be killed. Of course, she wouldn't care much for him thinking about keeping her safe, but it was hard for Barrett to fight his instincts to protect her.

Who the hell was doing this? And why? Barrett had to figure that it was connected to Casto and Alice, but that didn't give the reason why someone was now trying to kill Della and him.

Especially Della.

It certainly had him rethinking if his mother was behind this. Alice loved Della, and she wouldn't put her in danger. Of course, maybe Alice had lost control of any thug she might have hired to take care of her now dead lover. It could be that this had all gotten out of hand.

Despite the barrage of shots and his heartbeat drumming in his ears, Barrett managed to hear something else between the blasts. A sort of creaking sound, and even though he couldn't be sure, he thought someone had opened the door of the SUV. If so, that meant the shooter could be coming closer to them.

Trying to go in for kill shots.

"I have to get us out of here," Barrett said, and while keeping hold of his gun, he threw the truck into Reverse and hit the accelerator. The wet road didn't give him the safest surface to speed away, but he didn't have a lot of options here.

The shots continued to come at them, and when Barrett had some distance between them and the SUV, he spotted the gunman. A big bulky shouldered man he didn't recognize. The guy got off a few more shots while he jumped back into the SUV. The moment he was inside, the driver turned his vehicle toward them and came after Barrett's truck.

Barrett cursed because he was clearly at a disadvantage. The broken glass on the windshield cut his visibility. Plus, he was driving backward. The SUV had no such limitations and quickly ate up the distance between them.

"I'll try to stop them," Della insisted.

She didn't wait for Barrett to respond. Della came off the seat, her Glock already aimed, and she fired. Her shots blasted into the SUV windshield, shattering the safety glass as effectively as the gunman had done to Barrett's truck. It didn't slow down the driver, though. He continued to speed toward them, and he bashed the SUV into the truck's front bumper.

The jolt knocked Della and him around like rag dolls, causing her to fly back against the seat. It nearly caused Barrett to drive into the ditch, too, but he recovered as fast as he could, and he sent two shots into the SUV. It swerved. Not enough, though. And the driver made a quick correction to keep coming at them.

Worse, the shooter's hand snaked out again from the passenger's side window.

The gunman returned fire, and while at least one of the bullets missed, one slammed into the truck's side mirror right next to Barrett. Another landed somewhere near Della. Barrett couldn't risk checking to make sure she was okay. He had to focus on keeping them on the road so he could get them the hell out of there.

"We can't have them drive into Mercy Ridge," Della muttered.

Barrett was right there on the same page with her. No way did he want to lead these thugs into town where innocent bystanders could be shot. Unfortunately, Barrett couldn't just turn around and have the gunman chase them somewhere else. That meant he had to try to get the truck onto a side road or trail so that Della and he could make a stand.

"Try to call for backup," Barrett told her.

Della fumbled to get her phone from the equipment bag she had with her, and she sent off a text to someone. The second she finished, she levered herself up again. And she fired. She didn't miss, either. The two bullets blasted into the SUV's windshield, and the driver swerved again and slammed on the brakes.

The SUV went into a skid, but Barrett ignored it and kept trying to put some distance between them and his truck. Della didn't let up, either. She sent three more shots into the other vehicle.

Barrett finally saw what he'd been looking for. An old ranch trail that was wide enough for him to use. He had to brake as well so he could back into it as fast as he could. He threw the truck into Park, freeing up his hands so he could do his own shooting into the SUV.

The gunman ducked back inside the vehicle and, mimicking what Barrett had done moments earlier, the driver put pedal to the metal and started speeding backward. Away from Della and him. Barrett felt a split second of relief that they were no longer under fire. But it didn't last. He couldn't let these thugs get away because they could just lie in wait and attack them again.

"Hold on," Barrett warned Della, and he took off after the SUV. "How far out is backup?" he added when he heard her phone ding.

Della glanced down at the screen. "A minute, maybe less. However long it takes Jace to get here from the hospital."

Jace. Of course, she'd texted him. Then again, it was possible she didn't have the numbers for his brother or the other Mercy Ridge deputies.

Ahead of them, the SUV's brakes squealed, and Barrett saw the driver start turning the vehicle around. No doubt so they could try to speed away. But they clearly weren't giving up on killing them because the shooter's hand came out again, and the guy sent three back-to-back shots at them.

Despite the driver's maneuvering, the shots were dead-on.

One of them smacked right into Barrett's steering wheel, just inches from his hand, and he didn't want to know how close it'd come to his head. He didn't have time to worry about that, though, because he heard the sharp sound that Della made.

The sound of pain.

Barrett risked looking at her, and he saw something he definitely didn't want to see. Blood on her arm.

"Oh, God," she said, the words fighting with her gusting breath. "I need you to take me to the hospital now. I've been shot."

Chapter Five

Della forced herself to slow her breathing. Panicking wouldn't help and would only make things worse. Still, it was hard to hold it together when she felt the pain stabbing through her and saw the blood.

The baby.

The fear of losing her child roared through her like an unstoppable train barreling at her. The injury wasn't that serious. Definitely not life-threatening. But any loss of blood could also mean a miscarriage.

Della nearly blurted out for Barrett to hurry, that it wasn't just her arm injury at stake, but there was no need. Barrett was already hurrying, driving as fast as he safely could, and he was doing that while on the phone with Daniel to get his brother and a team out looking for that SUV. And for the men who'd just tried to kill them.

For as long as she could remember, she'd

wanted to be a cop. And wearing the badge meant facing danger just like this. But everything was different now that her baby was added to the mix. She couldn't lose his child. It didn't matter that the pregnancy hadn't been planned or that Barrett didn't want to be a father. She had to be okay so that her baby would be, too.

She managed to text Jace, to tell him that Barrett and she were heading back to the hospital and that he should do the same. Especially since Daniel would have the pursuit of the gunmen under control. Besides, she wanted Jace at the hospital in case those thugs came after Alice.

"How bad are you hurting?" Barrett asked when he ended the call with Daniel.

Della shook her head, hesitating so that she could try to get control of her voice. "It's okay."

It wasn't, of course. There was pain, but if she tried to describe it to Barrett, she might spill all about the baby. This wasn't the way she wanted him to find out. Later, after she'd been examined. Maybe after the shooters had been caught, she'd tell him then.

Thankfully, they weren't that far from the hospital, only a few minutes, and when Barrett pulled into the parking lot, he drove straight to the doors of the ER. Someone had alerted them, probably Daniel, because the moment Barrett came to a stop, a nurse and an EMT came rushing out toward them. Even though Della could have walked on her own, they put her on a gurney and rushed her into the hospital.

Barrett was right behind them.

There was no sign of Jace, but it was possible he hadn't made it back yet. That wouldn't last long. Della would have texted Jace about the shooting, and he would come to the ER to check on her.

It only took seconds for Dr. Tipton to hurry into the examining room with her, and Della didn't think it was her imagination that he seemed relieved when he saw her injury. Yes, there was blood running down the sleeve of her shirt, but it was all on her arm.

"Cut off her shirt," Tipton told the nurse. According to her name tag, she was Gayla Hayward.

Getting her out of her shirt would be just the beginning, Della knew. She'd likely need stitches, and for that to happen, Dr. Tipton would want to administer some kind of painkiller. That meant she'd need to tell him about the pregnancy.

"Could you please wait outside?" Della asked Barrett.

He blinked, maybe surprised that she didn't want him to see her partly undressed, and that's what Della wanted him to believe. For now, anyway.

"This shouldn't take long," Della added, "and I want an update on anything that Daniel and the others might have found. Plus, Jace will need to know."

Barrett hesitated, studying her face. Maybe trying to suss out why she was lying to him. But he finally got moving when the nurse cut away Della's blouse, leaving her bare to the waist except for her bra.

A black lace one.

It was barely there and more suited for date night than a police op, but it'd been the first thing Della had grabbed when she'd gotten dressed.

"If I'd known I was going to get shot, I would have worn something…more sensible," she muttered.

She hadn't intended for Barrett to hear that, but obviously he did, and despite their situation, the corner of his mouth lifted for just the briefest of smiles. Without saying anything to her, he walked out, shutting the door of the examining room behind him.

"It's a deep gash," Dr. Tipton immediately told her. He likely would have continued with an explanation of treatment, but Della caught onto his arm, turning him so they'd have eye contact.

"I'm pregnant," she whispered. The words sounded so foreign, and she realized why. It was the first time she'd said them aloud. "I haven't had an exam, but I've done pregnancy tests. They were positive."

Dr. Tipton stared at her, maybe piecing together why she'd sent Barrett out of the room. After all, it wasn't a secret that Barrett and she had been lovers. Of course, the doctor could think that she'd gotten pregnant after the breakup.

"How far along do you think you are?" Tipton asked.

"Two months," she answered without hesitation. It wasn't hard for her to remember that since she'd almost certainly gotten pregnant right before she'd ended things with Barrett.

Dr. Tipton nodded. "All right. I'd like to do another test here to confirm it, and I won't use any medication that could harm the baby."

The relief came but only as a trickle. There was a bigger concern here. "What about the blood loss?"

"Obviously, it's not ideal for an expectant mother to be shot, but it should be fine."

More than a trickle of relief that time. It came as a flood, and Della lay back on the table. "I don't want anyone else to know about the baby," she murmured.

"No one will hear it from us." Dr. Tipton began to gently press her stomach while the nurse took over cleaning her arm. "But if you're already two months, you won't be able to keep it a secret for long. And you shouldn't be doing duty that puts you in the line of fire."

Yes to both, and Della was trying to figure out how she would deal with that when she heard voices. Jace and Barrett. She didn't know what they were saying, but judging from the volume and tone, they were arguing.

On a heavy sigh, Della got up from the table, grabbed her cut-up shirt and held it in front of her while she opened the door. "I'm okay," she told Jace.

Jace didn't take her word for it. What else was new? He went to her, combing his gaze over her face, then her arm. Behind him, Barrett was doing the same thing, and Della hoped she looked stronger than she felt. Right now, she was shaken and feeling the nerves in every inch of her body.

A muscle flickered in Jace's jaw. "I'm going after the SOB who did this."

"Good." Della wanted that. Not just for her baby's safety but for anyone else who got in those thugs' line of fire. "It shouldn't take me long to get stitched up, and then I can help." Not with going out on patrol. No way would Jace allow that with her hurt. "I can make calls, check on the APB out on the gunmen."

"You can start with getting some rest when you're done here," Jace countered. "I don't want you to go home."

They were in agreement on that. "I could probably find a place to crash here. That way, I could keep an eye on Alice. How is she?" Della added.

Jace took a deep breath before he answered. "She's got a concussion so they're going to keep her overnight. There'll be a deputy or guard on her door." He paused, that jaw muscle working again. "Barrett and I will work that out."

In other words, there'd be a jurisdiction argument. Perhaps a very brief one, though, since Barrett had to be shorthanded what with so many of his deputies working the crime scene and going after those gunmen.

"Did Barrett tell you that we saw Wilbur Curran hanging in the hospital parking lot?" Della asked Jace.

"Not yet," Barrett provided. He might have said more, but the doctor interrupted them.

"Della needs that wound tended to," Dr. Tipton reminded them. "You'll have to talk later."

She nodded, gave Barrett and Jace what she hoped were reassuring looks and closed the door. Obviously, the two lawmen had some things to work out, and despite their checkered past, they would do what was best for this investigation.

Della returned to the table and tried to block out having her arm cleaned, then stitched. It hurt, but she had no intention of asking for pain meds. She'd read a few articles about pregnancy and knew that most meds in this early stage were a no-no. Of course, so was being in the crosshairs of a gunman. To make sure that didn't happen again, she'd have to work with Barrett. Because someone obviously wanted them dead.

But why?

The latest attack had to go back to Casto's murder and the assault on Alice, and it likely wasn't just a matter of killing anyone in law enforcement who might be investigating what happened in the woods. If so, the deputies and the CSIs at the crime scene would have come under fire. That meant Barrett and she were target specific. Someone wanted to eliminate them.

Which would eliminate her baby, too.

The thought of that felt like a meaty fist squeezing around her heart. It was also a reminder that she not only had to work with Barrett, she also had to tell him about the baby. Jace would help her stay safe, but once Barrett knew she was pregnant, it would be a huge distraction for him. For her as well, since she'd also have to deal with the backlash of whatever Barrett felt over having fatherhood thrust on him like this. After all, he'd made it clear that he'd never wanted children because of the ordeal he'd been through as a kid.

That felt like another squeeze around her heart.

She wanted this child, but she had to accept that Barrett might never feel the same way.

When the nurse was finished with the stitches, she drew a blood sample, which she explained would be used for a pregnancy test. Della was certain it would be another positive. However, it was probably best for her to wait for the results before she told Barrett. That might be chicken on her part, but she was too wrung out to deal with that upheaval tonight.

"You can take Tylenol," the doctor added as he helped Della off the examining table. The nurse handed her a green scrub top to wear. "If the pain gets too bad, come back in."

She hoped that wouldn't be necessary, but with or without the pain, Della wasn't expecting to have a restful night. Not with the nightmarish memories of the attack still firing through her mind.

Della thanked the doctor and nurse, put on the scrub top and went back into the waiting room, where she found Barrett pacing and talking on the phone. He was also sporting a very steely expression. He didn't aim it at her exactly, but she had no trouble seeing the questions in his eyes.

"I'm fine," she told him the moment he ended the call. Della glanced around but didn't see anyone else in the immediate area. "Where's Jace?"

"He got called back to his office. He said to remind you that he wants you to stay here, but if you insist on leaving, let him know, and he'll come and get you."

Jace's offer wasn't exactly a surprise, but Barrett continued before Della could say anything.

Barrett huffed, rubbed his hand over his face. "I want you to come back to my place. It's a lot closer than you going back to Culver Crossing, and I'd rather you not be out on the roads any longer than necessary."

The way he'd braced himself, it was as if he was preparing for an argument. But Della had no intention of doing that.

She nodded. "Thanks."

His braced stance continued, and this time there were more than questions in his eyes. There was suspicion.

"I'm tired," Della said, hoping that it would explain why she would readily agree to go to her ex-lover's house. And that was the truth. However, if the pregnancy test results came through by morning, she wanted to be able to tell Barrett where they'd have some privacy.

Barrett nodded as well, and he took out his phone again to fire off a text. "I'm having one of the deputies bring us a cruiser. My truck is too shot up to drive."

With everything else going on, Della had actually forgotten about that, but he was right. There hadn't been much left of the windshield. Plus, the cruiser would be bullet resistant.

"We got an ID on the dead man," Barrett said, putting his phone back in his pocket.

That got her attention, because this was almost certainly the person who kidnapped Alice. And the one who killed Casto.

"The guy had a record," Barrett went on, "so that's why they were able to ID him so fast. His name is Harris LeBeau."

Judging from the way Barrett was looking at her, he expected her to recognize the name. She didn't. "Who is he?"

"Along with being a former bouncer at a club, he also worked for Wilbur Curran," Barrett finally added.

Della pulled back her shoulders. She definitely didn't like that association, since Curran was likely as dirty as they came. Too bad Barrett didn't have proof of that.

"What did LeBeau do for Curran?" she asked.

"Personal security." Barrett punctuated that with a *yeah-right* sound.

She agreed with his skepticism. Personal security sounded more like hired muscle to her.

"Unfortunately, LeBeau officially quit working for Curran about two years ago." Barrett stopped, made a frustrated sigh. "In other words when I bring Curran in for questioning in the morning, he'll claim that he's had no recent association with the man."

Oh, yes. That's exactly what Curran would say. But it didn't make it true. "Maybe Curran will slip up during the interview. You could even ask him what he was doing here at the hospital tonight." Though she was betting Curran would have an explanation for that, too.

Barrett's phone rang, and his forehead bunched up when he saw what was on the screen. "Unknown caller," he said, putting the call on speaker.

Della's heart started to rev because she thought this might be the shooter contacting them. Obviously, Barrett had considered that as well, and he hit the record function on his phone before he answered it.

"Sheriff Logan?" the caller said. It was a woman, and Della instantly recognized the voice.

"Lorraine Witt," Della provided in a whisper to Barrett.

He shook his head, probably because he didn't know her. "Yes, I'm Sheriff Logan," Barrett answered. "Who is this?"

"I'm Lorraine Witt." Her sob came through loud and clear. "I just heard Robert Casto's been killed. Please tell me that's wrong. Please tell me he's alive." That was followed by another sob.

"How do you know Casto?" Barrett asked.

It took Lorraine several seconds to answer, and it sounded as if she was crying. "He's my lover...*was* my lover," she amended. "Is he really dead?"

"Yes, he's dead. He was murdered earlier this evening." Barrett paused a moment, no doubt to give Lorraine some time to absorb what he'd just told her. The woman wasn't absorbing it well, and the crying only got louder. "Who told you about his death?"

Lorraine didn't give an immediate answer, and when she did, her voice was clogged. "A friend, Jessa Marks. She called me. But I didn't believe her. I *can't* believe her. I loved Robert."

Barrett lifted an eyebrow, turning that silent question to Della. Had Casto been involved with both Alice and Lorraine at the same time? Della had to nod. Barrett huffed, muted the call.

"Casto and Lorraine have been on-and-off lovers for years," Della explained. "It's possible Casto was two-timing your mother."

"Great," Barrett grumbled. "Nothing like adding a love triangle to the mix of a murder investigation." He unmuted his phone. "Miss Witt, do you know anything about Casto's death?"

Her response was another loud sob. "No. No," she repeated. "I have to go," Lorraine quickly added, and she hung up.

Barrett stared at his phone as if considering hitting redial, but he finally just ended the record function. "How well do you know her?" Barrett asked Della.

"Well enough. Culver Crossing isn't any bigger than Mercy Ridge, so you know how it is."

He made a sound to indicate that he did. In small towns like theirs, law enforcement got to know pretty much everybody.

"She's never been arrested, never caused any trouble," Della added. "But I can't personally vouch for her." Even if she had been able to do that, Barrett would almost certainly want to talk to Lorraine and anyone else who'd had recent contact with Casto. Jace would do that, as well.

Barrett's phone dinged, and he read what was on the screen. "The cruiser's here and parked just outside the doors. Are you done here?"

Della nodded and would have fallen in step

with Barrett, but someone called out to her. It was the nurse, Gayla Hayward. Gayla had already opened her mouth to say something, but she stopped when she spotted Barrett.

"Uh, I need to tell you something," Gayla said to Della. "In private."

Della's stomach dropped, and she prayed this wasn't going to be bad news about the baby. She went to the nurse, who then led her a few feet away from Barrett.

"Dr. Tipton wanted me to tell you that he'll call you in the morning with the pregnancy test results," the nurse whispered. She handed Della a small brown paper bag. "He also wanted you to have a bottle of prenatal vitamins that you should start right away if the test is positive. And you'll need to schedule an appointment with an OB, of course."

"Of course," Della repeated in agreement. It was something she should have already done, but the shock of the news had thrown her for a loop.

After Della turned away from the nurse, she saw that Barrett had his gaze nailed to her, and he slid suspicious eyes down to the bag she was holding. He didn't ask what was in it, thank goodness, because Della figured her lying skills wouldn't be up to par tonight. She also gave another mental thanks when Barrett motioned for her to follow him to the cruiser.

"Move fast," he reminded her, though Della had already intended to do just that.

Barrett opened the passenger's side door for her before he took the keys from his deputy, Scottie Bronson.

"You're sure you don't want me to follow you out to your place?" Scottie asked.

Barrett shook his head. It was no doubt tempting to take Scottie up on his offer, but there were so many other things the deputy could be doing. Such as finding out who was responsible for the attacks so they could put an end to the danger. Della was certain that's what Barrett and she would be doing.

Well, that and trying to pretend that the old attraction between them was old enough to be finished.

Della hurried into the cruiser, and the moment that Barrett was behind the wheel, he took off. Like Della, he also fired glances all around them, looking for any signs of the gunmen, but no one was around.

Both a blessing and a curse.

Part of her would have liked to confront whoever was after them since they had backup and could probably catch and arrest the guys. However, the serious downside to that would be putting the baby at risk.

Barrett didn't say a word as he navigated out of the hospital parking lot and onto the street. His ranch wasn't far, just a few miles outside of town, but it would probably seem like an eternity before they got there. Della slid her hand over her weapon and intended to keep it there until they were safely inside Barrett's house.

"All right," Barrett said, causing her to glance at him. "Are you going to tell me what's going on?"

Della's heart skipped a beat or two. "What do you mean?" she asked, hoping she sounded puzzled rather than scared of his question.

"You know what I mean." His gaze slashed to the bag that was now in her lap. "I want to know what's wrong, and I want to know *now*."

Chapter Six

Barrett didn't want to take his eyes off the road or their surroundings for too long, but he made sure he caught Della's expression after he'd just made his demand.

I want to know what's wrong, and I want to know now.

Along with looking as if he'd just pointed a gun at her, she quickly glanced away. Obviously dodging his gaze. "I'm worried about going to your place," she finally said after some very long moments.

Barrett opened his mouth to argue that wasn't it, but he stopped. Because maybe that's all there was to it. After all, Della had broken up with him, and it could be she didn't want to do anything that would hint at them getting back together.

Was that it?

If so, then Barrett hoped this unsettled twinge

inside him would soon go away. Still, he had a bad feeling that Della had just lied to him.

Barrett didn't press her, in part because he truly did need to focus on the drive and also because his phone rang. Daniel's name popped up on the screen, which meant this was a call he needed to take. Since he wanted to keep his hands free, he put the call on speaker.

"I just got off the phone with Wilbur Curran," Daniel said. "He'll be in your office at eight in the morning so you can interview him."

Good. If it hadn't been so late, Barrett would have pressed for that interview to happen now, but he'd need a clearer head before he dealt with the likes of Curran.

"FYI, Curran's pissed off," Daniel added. "I'm guessing that won't surprise you."

It didn't, and he made a sound to indicate that. "Did Curran happen to say why he was at the hospital tonight?" Barrett pressed.

"I asked, and he said he'd answer the question when his lawyer was present."

That figured. Curran loved to hide behind his attorneys. And that meant it would be a battle to get anything from him. Still, Curran could be a hothead so he might slip up.

Barrett ended the call and pulled into the driveway in front of his house. He got as close to the porch as possible, angling the cruiser to prevent Della from being out in the open any longer than necessary. He expected her to balk about that, to remind him that she was a cop and didn't need such kid glove treatment. But she didn't utter one word of protest.

"I've never slept in the guest room," she muttered.

Considering that she looked embarrassed over that comment, Barrett guessed she hadn't meant to say it aloud.

That unsettled twinge inside him went up a notch.

He stepped ahead of Della, unlocking the door and disarming the security system. Once he had her inside the house, he immediately reset it and went through the living room and into the kitchen so he could make sure the door there was locked. It was. He'd also check all the windows, but for now he wanted to get Della settled. If *settling* was possible, that is. She stood in the foyer, her nervous gaze darting around, looking at anything but him.

"I don't have any pajamas," he said. Something she no doubt knew since he slept commando. "But there'll be some T-shirts in my dresser. That'll work for tonight, and then tomorrow... Well, we can work out a better arrangement."

She nodded, paused as if she might finally tell

him what was bugging her. But she didn't. On a long breath, she started for the hall. "I'll grab a T-shirt and a shower. Good night, Barrett."

He took his own long breath and started checking the windows. His house wasn't that big, only two bedrooms, a home office, two bathrooms and an open living, dining and kitchen area. Definitely no frills, but he didn't have time for such things what with tending to his horses and being the sheriff.

He'd barely finished with his security check when he heard Della in the shower of the guest room. He also heard a vehicle approaching the house, and that put him on full alert. Drawing his gun, he went to the front window, bracing himself for the worst. But it was Leo.

Barrett waited until his brother was on the porch before he paused the security system and opened the door. Leo stepped in, his attention going straight to Barrett's weapon.

"Just wanted to check on you," Leo said, his words trailing off when he heard the shower. "And Della. How is she?"

The hell if Barrett knew, but because he didn't want to discuss unsettled twinges with his brother, he just answered, "I think she's as all right as anyone can be who just got shot."

Leo nodded, paused and then cursed softly.

"This is a mess. You think Alice had something to do with Casto's murder?"

"She's connected. But I don't know how. *Yet*," Barrett added.

He understood all the things his brother wasn't saying. Leo was the baby of the family, and while he hadn't actually seen their father's dead body on the floor after he'd taken his life, that didn't mean he hadn't been just as traumatized as Barrett had been. Or Daniel. They'd all been cut to the core after their father's death, and that had all started with Alice. Now the woman was back in their lives, and this time they wouldn't be able to ignore her or pretend she didn't exist.

"If Alice isn't released from the hospital in the morning, I'll go there and have another chat with her," Barrett continued. "I need to ask her if she knows anything about the dead guy, Le-Beau."

That was for starters anyway. Barrett wanted a lot more details about the argument she'd had with Casto.

"I've put out feelers to a few criminal informants I know," Leo explained. "We might get lucky and find some proof that Curran hired LeBeau."

Yeah, that would indeed take some luck since Curran would have covered his tracks. If he was responsible for this, that is. The problem would be that Barrett wasn't even sure there was a connection between Casto and Curran, so why would Curran have hired someone to kill him? Unless this was all about setting up Alice. If that was it, then it wasn't a good way to get back at Barrett.

Maybe to get back at Della, though.

And that led Barrett to a question that he'd been mulling over. Had Della been the actual target? If so, why? He'd need to go over her recent cases to make sure this wasn't someone who was out for revenge.

Both Barrett and Leo turned at the sound of footsteps, and they saw Della coming toward them. She stopped as if frozen when she spotted Leo. Obviously, she hadn't expected his brother to be there. And Barrett hadn't expected to have the reaction he did to Della.

A *bad* one.

As he'd suggested, she was wearing one of his T-shirts, a nondescript gray one that was big on her. Still, it managed to skim her body in all the right places. Worse, it hit midthigh, showing plenty of her long legs. That caused his body to react, and it didn't seem to care that Della and he were no longer lovers.

"Sorry to interrupt," she said. "I heard you

talking to someone and wanted to make sure everything was okay."

Barrett nodded and would have likely said something had she not fluttered her hand toward the guest room and muttered a goodnight. Della turned and hurried off. The moment she was in the guest room, she shut the door.

Barrett took a moment, trying to rein in the heat that had roped and tied him up. Hell. He didn't want this; he didn't want Della, but apparently certain parts of him had other ideas.

"Are you okay with Della being here like this?" Leo asked, sliding him a glance.

Finally, that was an easy question to answer. No.

Barrett wasn't okay with it. Far from it. And he knew all the way to his gut that this was not going to end well.

DELLA SILENTLY CURSED the pain in her arm the next morning. And her headache. Since she was off both caffeine and meds, she couldn't do anything about either of them. She could only get dressed and hope that no one tried to kill her today.

Thankfully, there was a toothbrush and some toothpaste in the guest bath. A comb, too. That meant she could at least take care of minimal grooming, but she had no choice about putting her jeans and the scrub top back on. Which she did before making her way to the kitchen.

Barrett was there, of course, and he was also cursing. Not silently, though, as she was doing. He was muttering profanities while he read something on his laptop that he had on the breakfast nook table.

"Good," he said. "Glad you're up. I was about to knock on your door to tell you we'll need to leave soon for the interviews with Curran and Alice."

Those would be stressful. Maybe interesting, too, if Alice remembered anything else that would help them. The interviews also meant that she wouldn't be having that baby chat with Barrett this morning. Maybe after that, though, and she made a promise to herself that she wouldn't chicken out.

"The knife that killed Casto is still being analyzed, and the CSIs are going over the trace and fibers they took from the dead man's SUV," Barrett grumbled, sparing her a glance. "No sign of the two thugs who attacked us." Then, he cursed again when he glanced into his coffee cup. Probably because the caffeine wasn't working.

Of course, caffeine had big shoes to fill if it was to overcome some serious lack of sleep. And Della knew for a fact that Barrett had had as restless a night as she had, because she'd heard him moving around in his room. She'd moved, too, and hurt... Even with the pain she hadn't been able to forget that Barrett was just across the hall. Much too close for her body to forget.

She could say the same now.

It was déjà vu being in his kitchen like this, something that had happened many times when they'd been lovers. They'd had plenty of postsex mornings while they'd discussed the investigations into Francine's murder, Curran's money laundering and any others they were dealing with. They'd been good mornings, and Della missed being with him. Heck, she missed the sex. But she wasn't a fool, and she seriously doubted they could get back to that easy pace.

"There's coffee," Barrett added, tipping his head to the pot.

Since she didn't want him asking why she was skipping her usual cup, she laid her purse/equipment bag on the counter, went to the fridge and got some juice instead. No morning sickness, thank goodness, but she didn't want to risk eating right now.

"Leo didn't stay the night?" she asked.

Barrett shook his head and finally looked at her. He nearly did a double take, and at first she thought that was because she looked a wreck.

The pain had to be etched on her face. But there was something else in his smoky gray eyes. Heat. For her. It nearly caused Della to smile in a misery-loves-company sort of way, since there was no doubt some heat in her own eyes.

She considered just blurting out she was pregnant. That would not only cool the fire, but it would get this monkey off her back. But Barrett spoke before she could say anything.

"Jace texted me about an hour ago," Barrett explained. "He had one of his deputies bring you some clothes and toiletries to the sheriff's office."

Della hadn't expected Jace to do that but was glad he had. It did make her wonder, though, why Jace hadn't messaged her. Maybe he hadn't wanted to risk waking her. As if.

Barrett checked his watch. "If you want to grab something to eat—"

"I'm fine. We can go ahead and leave. If I get hungry, I can have the diner deliver something."

She had already put on her holster and gun, and the prenatal vitamins were in her bag. No way did she want to leave those lying around for Barrett to find if things worked out that she didn't come back here.

When they reached the door, Barrett motioned for her to stay back while he glanced around the yard. She immediately spotted

Buddy Adler, Barrett's part-time ranch hand, who was by the pasture fence. Buddy gave them a thumbs-up, probably a signal to Barrett that he hadn't seen anyone on the grounds. Good. She hadn't known Buddy would be around, but Della welcomed all the help they could get. Plus, Buddy was a reserve deputy so he could add an extra layer of security.

Barrett and she hurried into the cruiser, and she tried not to wince when the seat belt rubbed her arm. Tried and failed. And Barrett noticed.

"Didn't the nurse give you some pain meds?" he asked.

Since she didn't want to outright lie, she settled for saying, "I don't like taking them."

"I get that, but it'll be hard for you to focus on the interviews if you're hurting."

So true. Still, she didn't have another option. But it occurred to her that Barrett did—about the interviews anyway.

"Did Jace ask you to let me talk to Alice and Curran?" she pressed.

That tightened Barrett's jaw a little. "He brought it up."

Ah, she got it then. Jace had likely said he'd allow her to sit in or that he'd be the one to accompany Barrett. No way would her boss want to be left out of this, since the jurisdiction lines were blurred on this investigation.

Barrett didn't add anything else, and Della didn't push. She needed to aim all her mental energy at making it through this morning and dealing with the flashbacks she was having from the attack. Dealing with the worries, too, about the baby. She wished now that she'd asked the doctor more questions about how the stress could affect the pregnancy.

That last worry stayed in the forefront of Della's mind all the way to the sheriff's office. Leo must have been expecting them because he stepped out, keeping watch, until they were all in the building. Then, he handed her a small overnight bag that he picked up from a desk.

"From your boss," Leo said.

Della took the bag to the small bathroom just up the hall, and she was pleased when she saw that Jace had been thorough. She was also a little weirded out that he, or one of the other deputies, had had to go through her underwear. Still, she had fresh clothes to put on so she couldn't gripe about it. She also hurriedly put on some makeup since she was way too pale. Maybe some cosmetics would prevent people from asking her if she was okay.

The moment she stepped out of the bathroom, Della heard the booming voice, and she followed it to Barrett's office. Wilbur Curran was there. And she automatically scowled. So did Curran, and he aimed that particularly acid expression at both Barrett and her.

Curran wasn't alone, of course. There were two suits with him. Lawyers, no doubt, though she didn't recognize either of them. No suit for Curran. He was wearing pricy jeans and a brown leather vest over a crisp white shirt.

"Well, this is an unholy alliance," Curran commented, keeping his scowl on Della. "I didn't know you'd started crawling back into the sheriff's bed."

Della met him eye to eye. "You've obviously got a lot of spare time on your hands if you're keeping up with my personal life."

His jaw tightened, and he opened his mouth, likely to snap back at her, but one of the suits stepped between them. "I'm Gene Templeton, and this is Blaine Conway. We're representing Mr. Curran and ask that you direct any and all comments and questions to us."

Yep, Curran had thrown up that legal wall again. One that Barrett ignored when he looked directly at Curran. "Come with us now."

Barrett didn't wait to see if his order would be met. He just started up the hall toward the interview room. Della followed, and after a whispered conversation with his lawyers, the trio joined them.

When they were all inside and seated, Barrett turned on the recorder, read Curran his rights and then named everyone in the room so it would be part of the official record.

"This is getting real old, real fast," Curran said the moment Barrett finished. "When are you going to get tired of trying to pin stuff on me?"

"I don't get tired of doing my job," Barrett fired back. "I need your whereabouts last night."

The lawyers, who were seated on both sides of Curran, leaned in as if to whisper something, but Curran answered. "At home and then at the hospital. Because you saw me there, that makes you and Deputy Delish here my alibis."

Since Curran had called her that to get a rise out of her, Della didn't accommodate him. She calmly set her bag on the floor next to her, gave him a flat stare and let Barrett continue to take the lead on the interview.

"Home?" Barrett challenged. "Can anyone verify that?"

Curran smiled. It was slick and oily. "Of course, a couple of my ranch hands saw me. I can give you their names."

"Do that." Barrett slid a tablet of paper his way, though both Della and he knew that anyone who worked for Curran would also lie for him. "Why were you at the hospital last night?"

"Just being nosy." Curran grinned. "I heard

that your mama was brought in, and I wanted to see if I could hear any gossip."

That was possibly the truth. *Possibly*. It was also possible Curran had wanted to pump someone for info to see if the murder could be connected to him.

Barrett added a few more questions about the hospital visit, nailing down times. Or rather the times that Curran admitted to.

"Tell me about Harris LeBeau," Barrett threw out there.

Now the lawyers moved in again, and the whispering ensued. Curran, however, nailed his attention to Barrett, and the man appeared to be fighting a smile. A reaction that he might hope would rile Barrett and her. That's why Della returned the half smile while making sure her eyes were all cop. That shut Curran down.

"LeBeau used to work for me," Curran snapped, while his lawyers were still whispering. "As I'm sure you already know. You also know that I ended that employment two years ago."

"When's the last time you saw him?" Barrett fired back.

Curran lifted his shoulder. "A couple of months ago. I saw him at a club in San Antonio. Or maybe it was Austin. We didn't speak," he added with his poker face back in place.

"You're sure about that?" Barrett, again.

"Think hard because I'm looking for witnesses now who can tell me otherwise. If I find one person, *just one*, who saw you exchange a single word, then I'll be able to arrest you for giving a false statement and obstruction of justice."

That got the lawyers started, and they doled out their own threats of harassment. Curran's poker face vanished, and the anger flared through his dust-gray eyes. "LeBeau and I didn't talk," he insisted over his lawyers' objections.

Barrett gave Curran a very skeptical look. "Did you know that LeBeau's dead?"

"Yeah. I heard about that," Curran confirmed. "People in this town just love to talk."

Della couldn't dismiss the gossip factor. It could be how Curran had heard the news, but she was betting Curran still had contacts who'd fed him such information.

"As usual, Sheriff, you're barking up the wrong tree," Curran added a moment later. "If you want to find out who's trying to kill the deputy and you, then you need to take a closer look at your own gene pool."

Barrett leaned back in his chair, stared at Curran. "What do you mean?" Barrett asked.

"Well, I'm not responsible for LeBeau's and Casto's deaths, but I'm pretty sure I know who is." Curran smiled. "You need to be talking to your mother."

Chapter Seven

His mother.

Of course.

Barrett had wondered how long it would take Curran to fan some flames by bringing Alice into this. That said, maybe there was some truth to what he'd just said. And it was because of that possible truth that Barrett figured the interview with Alice would go past the point of just being uncomfortable. Then again, things were never comfortable when it came to his mother.

"Do you have proof that Alice had anything to do with the two murders and the attack?" Della snapped, her narrowed eyes latched to Curran's.

Curran shrugged as if this were a friendly chat. "It just seems obvious to me. After all, Alice had a spat with Casto not long before he was killed. Don't you law enforcement types always look at the spouse or lover?" He threw that out with plenty of smugness but then paused.

"But Alice doesn't seem to have the stomach for stabbing and shooting, does she?" His gaze shifted back to Barrett. "Her specialty is doing stuff to others to make them end their lives."

Barrett wished that arrow hadn't found its mark, but it did. Always would. Because it didn't matter how many years had passed, Barrett would never forget his father's suicide. Would also never forget that Alice had brought him to that fatal brink. However, Barrett was old enough, *now*, to accept that the suicide hadn't actually been Alice's fault.

"Come to think of it," Curran went on, "Alice would have needed help for something like this."

Della huffed. "You're saying Alice hired Le-Beau?"

Curran made a humming sound as if giving that some thought. "No, hiring someone like LeBeau isn't her style, either. But she could have teamed up with Casto's other woman." He chuckled. "Now, Lorraine Witt's got a hot enough head to help Alice do something like this."

Barrett thought of Lorraine's frantic phone call the night before. Not hotheaded then but very worried. She hadn't sounded like a woman scorned as much as someone devasted by losing the man she loved. Still…

"How do you know Lorraine?" Barrett asked Curran.

Curran blinked as if surprised by the question. "I've met her a few times, and I've heard plenty of things about her. Your mama might have that whole 'still waters run deep' thing going on, but Lorraine wears her heart on her sleeve. She might have gotten fed up with Casto's bed hopping and convinced Alice that he had to die."

Or maybe Lorraine had done this on her own. Barrett didn't know a lot about the woman, but that would soon change. He texted Daniel to do a background check on Lorraine and to have her come in ASAP for questioning. Daniel texted back that he would arrange it and ended the message with:

Alice's injuries apparently weren't serious so she was released from the hospital. She's here.

That was as good a reason as any for Barrett to wrap up this interview with Curran. He didn't think he was going to get anything more from the man, and if something came up in his financials check, he could always bring Curran back in. Of course, Curran would claim that was harassment, but Barrett didn't care. The images of the blood on Della's arm was much too vivid to care about anything other than keeping her safe and getting to the bottom of what was going on.

"You can go," Barrett said, standing.

He considered adding that he would get a warrant for Curran's financials, just to see how the man would react, but it would likely only cause some outrage and blustering about more harassment. Barrett would get the warrant, would dig deep into it and hope that he found a money trail.

Barrett and Della stayed put while Curran and his lawyers left. He figured Della would need a quick breather before facing Alice, but one look at her, and Barrett knew it might take a heck of a lot longer than a moment. Della was way too pale.

"Is your arm hurting?" he quickly asked.

She shook her head, and he could see her trying to steel herself up. Cursing under his breath, Barrett went to her. To do what, he didn't know, but apparently it was going to be his day for stupid things, because he touched her, putting his fingers under her chin to lift it and force eye contact. He didn't like what he saw there.

"Why don't you let me get your pain meds, the ones the nurse gave you last night?" he pressed.

Della gave another shake of her head, which caused his fingers to slide against her skin. And just like that, Barrett had memories of a different kind. Bad ones. When he'd touched Della. When he'd kissed her.

Something his brainless body wanted to do right now.

Worse, he saw more than pain in her eyes. Barrett watched as that slow curl of heat washed over her face. Damn her.

Damn him.

He moved his hand higher, his thumb brushing over her bottom lip. Definitely not a smart thing to do, but he didn't stop, and Della didn't back away. In fact, she sort of moved into it, making it much more than a touch.

This was foreplay, and he was starting to have a lot of bad ideas that he shouldn't have. Thankfully, he was saved by the sound of footsteps. Someone was walking toward the interview room, and a moment later, Daniel appeared in the doorway.

His brother had obviously been about to say something, likely something that had nothing to do with why Barrett and Della looked as if they were guilty of a multitude of things, but Daniel just stood there a long moment. Staring at them. Maybe even waiting for them to explain why there was a scalding hot vibe in the air.

"What?" Barrett practically snapped to get his brother to stop gawking.

Daniel flexed his eyebrows, and Barrett hoped that wasn't amusement he was seeing on his brother's face. If it was, it didn't last. Daniel's expression went heart attack serious.

"You want me to bring in Alice, or do you need a…moment?" Daniel asked.

"Bring her in," Della and Barrett said in unison. Their tones and swift responses didn't make them appear less guilty.

Daniel nodded, then lingered a moment as if expecting some kind of explanation. One that Barrett was certain he wouldn't get. He finally turned and walked away.

Barrett knew he wouldn't have much time to steel himself up and cool down his body. Neither would Della, but she was dealing with a couple of other obstacles that Barrett didn't have.

The pain and Della's friendship with Alice.

A friendship that had developed because Alice and Della lived in the same small town. Probably also because Della felt sorry for Alice since she was estranged from her family. There was also the Jace factor. Alice had had some part in raising Jace so that meant Della had had opportunities to socialize with and also get close to Alice.

It wasn't easy to interrogate a friend, or a mother, but Barrett figured Della and he would do their best. After all, the danger could extend to Alice, too, and Della would want to do whatever it took to make sure the woman wasn't attacked again.

Part of him wanted to pawn this interview off onto someone else, but there wasn't anyone in his department who didn't have a personal opinion about Alice. And those opinions were negative. But Barrett knew he could be objective with the facts, and if he got into boggy ground and lost his objectivity, he'd be willing to ask the Rangers to send someone in to do a more thorough interview.

Barrett put a fresh notepad on top of the interview notes he had from Curran, and he'd just sat down when Daniel brought in Alice. She looked better than she had the night before but not much. There was a bandage on her head, and a nasty bruise ran from her right temple to her cheek.

"Barrett," Alice greeted, and she managed a smile. An uneasy one that turned more genuine when she looked at Della.

Alice went to Della, moving in as if she might give her a kiss on the cheek, but she stopped, her gaze sliding down to Della's badge that was hooked on her belt. His mother didn't seem to resent that Della was here in an official capacity. However, that badge had to be a reminder that this wasn't the place for hugs.

Something Barrett also needed to remember.

"Jace told me what happened, that someone fired shots at Barrett and you and that you were hit. Are you okay?" Alice asked Della.

Judging from Della's soft sigh, she was tired of hearing that question, but she gave Alice a reassuring nod. "And you?"

Alice touched her fingers to the bandage on her head. "We've both been better." She shifted her attention back to Barrett and then eased down into the chair across from him. That didn't stop her from volleying glances at Della and him. "Are...you two back together?"

Great day. Was he wearing a sign or something? Or maybe Alice just picked up on that same vibe Daniel had.

"No," Barrett answered, and he shifted things back to business. "You didn't bring a lawyer?"

"No." She paused, then softly repeated her answer. "I want to help. And I didn't do anything wrong," Alice insisted.

He could have spelled out that plenty of innocent people had lawyers accompany them to interviews. Plenty of guilty ones, too. Instead, Barrett just Mirandized her again to refresh her of her rights—one of which was for her to have an attorney present. The refresh wasn't legally necessary, but since she'd perhaps been in shock and suffering from her injury during the other reading, Barrett wanted to make sure the ground rules were clear.

"Go ahead, ask your questions," Alice said when he'd finished. "I want to find the person who tried to hurt Della and you."

Barrett noted that Alice had omitted herself from the "finding justice" vow. Casto, too. And that gave Barrett his starting point.

"Did you kill Robert Casto?" he came out and asked.

Alice's eyes widened, and she volleyed more glances at Della and him.

"I thought that man, Harris LeBeau, killed him." Alice's voice was shaky now. "That's what I heard some of the nurses talking about in the hospital."

"I need your answer for the record." He tipped his head to the recorder that he'd turned on. "Did you kill Robert Casto?"

"No, I didn't kill him," Alice said on a rise of breath, and she went from looking frazzled and timid to rattled. Of course, she'd been attacked, too, so maybe that was playing into this.

"You're positive?" Barrett pressed.

Alice paused. Way too long. So long that it caused him to groan. Alice groaned, too, and tears sprang into her eyes. "Some things are still hazy, and I just don't remember if I stabbed him." And with that, her breath broke in a sob. "But I couldn't have killed him. I'm sure I would have remembered that."

You'd think, but then there was the head injury. Barrett would need to talk to her doctor and find out if the injury could have caused memory loss or if that was just a convenient out. He was leaning toward the first one. Not because she was his mother—that didn't play in her favor here—but because it was what made sense. If she'd murdered Casto, he couldn't see her staying around and putting herself smack in the middle of a crime scene.

"Tell me about LeBeau," Barrett said, going for a different approach. "Did you know him?"

Alice grabbed a tissue from the box on the table and wiped her eyes. "Yes."

Barrett didn't know who was more surprised by her answer, Della or him. "How did you know him?" Della asked.

This time Alice didn't hesitate. "I met him at the cattleman's ball, the one that Robert hosted at his ranch about six months ago."

Now, that was an interesting connection. "Casto and LeBeau knew each other?" Barrett pressed.

"Oh, yes." But then she paused. "Robert had done some business with him." Another pause. "Come to think of it, they weren't exactly friendly that night, though, but I figure that's because of Lorraine."

Both Della and Barrett practically snapped to attention. "Lorraine Witt?" Della questioned.

Alice nodded, but then she must have noticed that they'd latched on to something. "Yes. Lorraine and Mr. LeBeau were once engaged."

EVEN WITH HER foggy head, Della could see how the pieces were fitting together. Curran was connected to LeBeau who was in turn connected to Lorraine—which made all of them connected to Alice.

And that in turn made Lorraine, Curran and, yes, Alice suspects in Casto's murder.

Della wanted to put Alice at the bottom of the suspect list, but there was a problem with that.

Some things are still hazy, and I just don't remember if I stabbed him.

Those were Alice's own words, and they could be used to incriminate her. Well, if any corroborating evidence came to light, it would. So far, there wasn't any, but it didn't look good that Alice had been found just yards away from her ex-lover's body. The Mercy Ridge DA could use that to charge her with murder. And that's why Della had to push the woman to do anything she could to clear her name.

Barrett wouldn't understand why she felt a connection with his estranged mother. But she did. The woman had always seemed so sad and lost as if she'd accepted there was nothing she could do to make up for her past. To add plenty more salt to the wound, Della knew Alice still loved her sons. Sons who'd likely never forgive her for what'd happened to their father. Yes, Alice had made a horrible mistake, but Della knew the woman paid for it with her bone-deep grief.

"Tell us more about Lorraine," Della said, figuring that Barrett wouldn't object if she launched into the interview.

Alice nodded, but it seemed to take her a moment to compose herself. "I'm sure you know that Lorraine is Robert's ex." She clamped her teeth over her bottom lip for a second. "And she wants…wanted him back. I could tell. I believe that's why she brought Mr. LeBeau with her to the cattleman's ball, so that she could maybe try to make Robert jealous."

"And was he jealous?" Barrett said when Alice didn't continue.

Alice cleared her throat, blinked back tears. "I'm pretty sure that Robert continued to see Lorraine, maybe even continuing his affair with her. He denied it, but she's one of the reasons we argued. That and he became so controlling."

That meshed with everything Della knew about Casto. Controlling and a cheat. That meant plenty of people could have wanted him dead.

"How much do you remember about last night?" Barrett asked her.

"Only what I've already told Jace and you," Alice insisted. "I remember a man grabbing me in my garage. Then, I woke up outside in the woods."

"No other fragments of memories of something that might have happened in between your being kidnapped and us finding you?" Barrett pushed.

Alice shook her head. "But the doctor said everything might come back. He said this happens sometimes with head injuries."

Della nodded. "Did the doctor mention you seeing a therapist? Maybe someone who could use hypnosis?"

"No." Some of the tension faded from Alice's face. "But I think that's a good idea. I want to remember. No matter what, I have to know."

So did Della and Barrett. Because if Alice hadn't killed Casto and LeBeau, then they could focus on Lorraine and Curran.

"Why don't you go ahead and make an appointment with a therapist," Barrett advised her, and then he glanced at his phone when it dinged. "And I'll want to interview you again."

"Of course," Alice said in a whisper. "You're not arresting me?"

The muscles in Barrett's jaw tightened. "Not at this moment. Once I've finished all the interviews and gotten reports back from the crime scene teams, I'll know whether or not I have probable cause to ask a judge for an arrest warrant."

Nodding, swallowing hard, Alice got to her feet when both Della and he did. Alice moved as if to leave, but then she turned back to Della. "You should get some rest. You look very tired."

Looking tired was the least of her worries. Della was dealing with the pain and the looming reminder that she had to tell Barrett about the baby. Maybe she could do that as soon as the first round of interviews were done.

Not here, though.

She'd need to find some place private for there would no doubt be fallout. Della had been stunned to learn about the pregnancy, but she'd had a day now to work through her feelings. Too bad she couldn't give Barrett that much time. He'd need it, but they'd have to jump back into the investigation.

She followed Alice to the door so she could say goodbye to the woman and try to give her a reassuring look. Della was certain that she failed. So did Alice, who offered her a watery smile in response.

"You're not driving yourself home, are you?" Della asked.

"No. Jace sent one of the deputies, and he's waiting out front for me."

Good. That was a reminder that she needed to thank Jace, something Della was certain that Alice had already done.

After Alice walked away, Della turned back to Barrett. He had gotten up from his seat, but he had his attention nailed to whatever he was reading on his phone.

"The lab reports from the CSIs," Barrett muttered without looking at her.

There was something in his body language that sent Della rushing to his side, and she soon saw that he'd scrolled through the bulk of the report. However, one thing did catch her eye.

Alice Logan's fingerprints.

Della could have sworn that her heart skipped a couple of beats, and she was still trying to tamp down the panic when Barrett turned to her.

"Alice's prints were in LeBeau's SUV," he said.

The relief came. That could mesh with Alice's statement about being kidnapped. Well, it would if LeBeau had been the one to kidnap her. But the concern quickly tamped down the relief. "Were her prints anywhere else?" And she prayed that Barrett didn't say they were on the murder weapon.

"Maybe." Barrett groaned after his answer. "There are fingerprint smears on the handle of the knife. Maybe Alice's, maybe someone else's. The lab has to do further testing."

So, Alice wasn't in the clear just yet, but since Della believed the woman was innocent, she also had to believe that the evidence would exonerate her. Well, it would unless the real killer had planted Alice's prints there. Considering everything else that'd happened, Della figured that's exactly what Casto's murderer had done.

Barrett and she looked up when they heard a woman's voice coming from the squad room. Not Alice's. But rather Lorraine Witt's.

"I want to see the sheriff now," Lorraine demanded. Judging from her tone, she seemed to think someone was going to prevent that, but Della and Barrett both wanted to see her—and question her.

Barrett stepped out, heading toward the squad room, and Della stayed put a moment to gather her breath. Surprisingly, the pain was somewhat better now, which was a good thing because she needed to focus on Lorraine.

"Why isn't Alice behind bars?" she heard Lorraine ask, and a moment later, both Barrett and the woman came into view. Lorraine was dressed to the nines, as she usually was, in a stylish blue dress that was nearly the same color as her eyes. She had her dark blond hair pulled back from her face. "It's obvious that Alice murdered Robert."

"That's far from obvious," Barrett muttered under his breath. Lorraine rolled over him, repeating her question about why he hadn't arrested Alice, and he read Lorraine her rights.

That stopped her, and Lorraine's eyes widened. "You're arresting me?" she snarled.

"Mirandizing you," Barrett corrected. "It's procedure, and it's for your own protection. I hope you caught the part about you having a lawyer present if you want."

"I don't need a lawyer. I'm innocent."

Della figured that Lorraine didn't know that Alice had said pretty much the same thing. But no lawyer was a good thing because it meant that Barrett and she could question the woman.

"First of all, I'll need your whereabouts for between 6:00 p.m. last night and one this morning," Barrett said.

Lorraine made a sound of outrage, but then she sank down into the chair across from Della and Barrett. "I was home, waiting for Robert.

He was supposed to come over, and when he didn't, I got very worried." She blinked back tears. "Obviously, I had a right to be worried. Robert's dead." Now some of those tears fell.

"Was anyone with you?" Barrett pressed. "I'll need someone to verify your alibi."

Lorraine's face didn't show as much outrage as Curran's had done, but it was close. "My housekeeper, Debra Wallace, was there."

Barrett passed her a notepad. "Give me her contact info so I can call her."

That dried up the rest of Lorraine's tears, and when she wrote down the housekeeper's name and phone number, the pressure from her grip caused the pen to dig into the paper.

"There," Lorraine snapped when she was done. She passed the tablet back to him. "Now that we have that out of the way, I want you to tell me what you're doing to bring Robert's killer to justice."

"I'm questioning any and all persons of interest," Barrett calmly replied, keeping his cop's stare on Lorraine. "Did you murder Casto?"

"No!" Lorraine practically shouted that, but the burst of energy seemed to drain her, and she dropped her head in her hands. "No," she repeated in a much calmer voice. "I was in love with him."

"You loved him even though he was seeing another woman?" Barrett asked.

"Robert didn't love Alice," she quickly answered. "The fact that he continued to see me proves that."

Not really. It only proved that Casto was a womanizer.

"What he felt for Alice was just an infatuation, that's all," Lorraine added. "And he'd already ended things with her. That's why Alice killed him. If she couldn't have him, then she decided no one else would."

"That could be a motive for murder," Della pointed out. "But there's that old adage about a woman scorned. That could apply to both Alice and you which means you have motive, too."

Oh, Lorraine didn't care for that. If looks could have killed, Lorraine would have blasted Della to smithereens.

"I wasn't scorned," Lorraine said through now clenched teeth. "Robert always came back to me, and he would have done that again if Alice hadn't murdered him."

"Tell me about Harris LeBeau," Barrett interrupted, causing Lorraine to shift her scowl from Della to him.

Lorraine pulled back her shoulders. "He's dead. Alice killed him, too."

"Tell me about him," Barrett insisted. "I understand you were engaged to him."

"Yes, years ago. That was long before Robert and I became involved."

Barrett glanced down at the notes he'd taken earlier. "Yet you attended a party with LeBeau about six months ago."

Lorraine obviously hadn't been expecting that, and she blinked in surprise. "That's right. It wasn't actually a date, though. I simply wanted an escort for the party, and he wanted to go."

"And you wanted an escort so you could make Casto jealous?" Barrett said, his tone and expression skeptical.

Lorraine's eyes narrowed. "No. There was no need for me to do that because Robert knew how much I loved him." She paused. "Alice told you about the party." Lorraine muttered some profanity under her breath and got to her feet. "Alice is obviously trying to set me up, and you're too biased to see that's what she's doing. This interview is over. If you have anything else to say to me, you can contact my attorney."

With that, Lorraine stood and stormed out the door. Della waited to see if Barrett was going to stop her. He didn't.

"I don't have any evidence I can use to hold her," he said, and it seemed to Della that he was talking more to himself than to her. "That might change when I dig into her financials. Of course, if she got LeBeau to kidnap Alice and kill Casto, LeBeau might have done it as a favor and not because she paid him."

"True." Della gave that some thought. "But Lorraine might have hired someone to kill Le-Beau. Maybe so he couldn't implicate her. If so, there might be a money trail for that."

Barrett nodded. "If you want to help look for that, I can find you a desk and a computer to use."

She was about to suggest they go back to his place and work there, so they could talk. But when she lifted her bag from the floor, the strap caught on the back of the chair, causing the contents to spill out onto the table. One item landed right on top of the others. And the label on the bottle was clearly visible.

Prenatal vitamins.

She reached to scoop it up, but it was already too late. Barrett had seen it, and his gaze sliced from the bottle to her.

"Della, are you pregnant?" Barrett demanded.

Chapter Eight

Barrett tried to rein in the storm of emotions rolling through him. And Della's stunned silence sure didn't help with that. If she wasn't pregnant, then a quick denial should have come out of her mouth, maybe followed by an equally quick explanation of why she had prenatal vitamins in her purse.

But that didn't happen.

Della's eyes widened, and her breath seemed to stall in her throat for a couple of long seconds. Then, he saw the answer in her eyes right before she said the single-word answer.

"Yes." Her voice had barely any sound, but Barrett heard it loud and clear.

His gaze automatically dropped to her stomach. No signs there that she was pregnant, but then he wasn't sure how far along a woman needed to be before she started to show. And then he said something that would change his life forever. The way it'd already changed Della's.

"It's my baby." Barrett's voice didn't fare much better than Della's, but he was damn lucky to have gotten out that handful of words.

Della nodded, but he hadn't needed her confirmation. He knew. Even though Della hadn't been in love with him, he had no doubts that he'd been her only lover for, well, years. Their friends with benefits arrangement had made it easy for them not to risk their hearts with someone else who would have demanded more than just sex.

"I know we always used a condom, but those apparently aren't foolproof. And now I'm two months pregnant," she added.

That sent a new slam of thoughts and emotions, and they raged through him like a fierce battle. Della was pregnant. *With his baby.* That meant he'd be the very thing he'd always sworn he wouldn't be.

A father.

Barrett figured he was going to have to come to terms with that. Soon. And he would, once he could actually think straight. But for now, there was a different concern, and it had to do with that bandage on her arm.

"The gunshot wound…" he managed to say.

She shook her head. "The doctor doesn't think it hurt the baby, but he's scheduled me for an ultrasound. He wants me to make an appointment with an OB, too."

He heard everything she said, her words echoing in his head, but Barrett latched on to the first part. *The doctor doesn't think it hurt the baby.* That was good. However, it wasn't nearly enough reassurance.

Barrett cursed. "I should have never had you in my truck, driving out to a crime scene."

Della shook her head again. "We were both doing our jobs."

That only caused him to curse even more. "You should have told me you were pregnant." But then Barrett paused. "Unless you didn't know then. When did you find out?"

Now it was Della's turn to hesitate. "I did some home tests yesterday. Before Casto was murdered." She swallowed hard. "The tests were all positive, and while I was at the hospital, the doctor did another test to confirm it."

So, Della had known before she'd responded to that anonymous text that had caused them to go into the woods.

"I'm sorry," she said. "Not sorry about the baby," Della quickly added, "but I'm sorry because I know this isn't what you want."

There it was. All spelled out for him. Except Della had it slightly wrong. After raising his brothers, Barrett had figured that he'd best keep fatherhood off the table. He hadn't failed exactly—both Leo and Daniel had turned out all right—but Barrett wasn't taking any of the credit for that.

His brothers had turned out all right *despite* him.

He'd made plenty of mistakes, as his own father had done, and that'd convinced him that it wasn't a good idea to create another generation of Logans.

"Give me a minute," he told her, putting his hands on his hips and dragging in several deep breaths. It didn't help. No surprise there. This was going to take more than some extra oxygen and a minute to process.

Della gave him that minute. Her eyes stayed locked on him, and she was doing some heavy breathing of her own. Plus, she winced during one of those breaths, and that was a reminder she was having to deal with this along with the aftermath of nearly being killed.

"Okay," Barrett finally said. Of course, it wasn't okay, far from it, but he thought he could finally form enough words to discuss this with her.

"Before you say anything else, I want you to know that I can do this pregnancy alone," Della interrupted. "If you want to be a part of this, fine, but if you don't, I'll understand."

For some reason her almost congenial offer riled him to the bone. They weren't discussing dinner plans here but rather something that would change everything forever.

"I'm already a part of this," he managed to say, though it was hard to speak through clenched teeth.

Barrett likely would have added a lecture about her not shutting him out even if he wasn't sure how he was going to deal with this, but the sound of footsteps stopped him. A moment later Daniel appeared in the doorway.

His brother had already opened his mouth to say something, but he stopped, no doubt picking up on a different vibe in the room. Not the old heat between Della and him. But rather their new situation that felt as if it could bring him to his knees. Barrett pushed all of that aside, though, for now, because it was obvious Daniel had something important to tell him.

"There's a problem," Daniel started, still eyeing them with plenty of concern. "Someone torched Alice's house."

Della gasped. "Is she okay?"

Daniel nodded, shifted his attention back to Barrett. "The fire department's already on scene, but according to the call I just got, there's plenty of damage. Too much for her to stay there. Oh, and because I know you'll ask,

Alice didn't do this. She was on her way home with a deputy."

Yeah, Barrett would have definitely asked about that, especially since there could have been something inside the house that Alice wouldn't want to come to light. The CSIs had already gone through the place, but they might have missed something. Plus, this could also make her look more like the victim that she appeared to be.

"I'm guessing no one saw who did this?" Barrett asked.

"Nope." Daniel gave a weary sigh. "Alice has ranch hands, but they were back in the pasture and didn't see anyone. There's more," he added, that weariness going up a notch. "The deputy who was driving Alice home says someone tried to run them off the road. Two men in an SUV. The deputy called for backup, but the men got away."

"Hell." That was likely the pair who'd tried to kill Della and him. "Please tell me the deputy got the license plate numbers?"

"He did, but they're bogus," Daniel answered.

Of course, they were. Hired killers weren't likely to advertise their identities by driving a vehicle that could be traced back to them.

"Alice is apparently pretty shaken up," Daniel went on. "So shaken up that the deputy is bringing her back here to the hospital." He checked his watch. "They should be arriving right about now. And she said she needs to talk to Della and you."

"Hell," Barrett repeated.

He scrubbed his hand over his face. The last thing he wanted right now was a conversation with his mother, but this could have something to do with the investigation. Maybe she had to tell them something that she didn't want to share with Jace's deputy.

Barrett knew he wasn't going to be able to push aside all thoughts of the pregnancy, but maybe this trip to the hospital could be a "kill two birds with one stone" kind of visit. He could talk to Alice. And confirm that Della's gunshot wound truly hadn't affected the baby. Of course, he wasn't sure what he would do with the info other than add another worry to his list, but he had to know.

"I can go with Della and you," Daniel offered.

But Barrett shook his head. "I want you to get on those financials. Both Lorraine's and Curran's. Run Casto's, too."

"You think Casto might have hired those thugs?" Daniel asked.

"Maybe." It was possible this was a situation of a hired hit gone wrong. If Casto had paid LeBeau and the two gunmen to go after Alice, then maybe the men had turned on him. Despite the old saying, Barrett hadn't found much honor among thieves. Or would-be killers.

Barrett started toward the front of the building where he'd left his cruiser, and Della was right behind him. He automatically slowed his steps, hoping it would stop her from wincing again from pain. But the wince happened anyway when she put on her seat belt in the cruiser.

"You can't take pain meds because of the baby," Barrett said more to himself than her.

"No. Well, not the pain meds that would actually do much good. It's okay," Della tacked on to that.

He wasn't sure about the okay part. Wasn't sure of much right now. However, Barrett shook his head to try to clear it and kept watch around them as he drove them to the hospital. It wasn't far, just up Main Street, and there weren't any strangers milling around. No vehicles that he didn't recognize, either. He was grateful for being in a small town where things like that stood out. Of course, one of their main suspects—Curran—wouldn't stand out, either, and Barrett suspected the man could be as dangerous and mean as a rattlesnake.

Barrett spotted the Culver Crossing cruiser just outside the ER doors, and he pulled to a stop behind it. No sign of the deputy, but he was likely with Alice. Barrett hoped so anyway. If someone truly wanted her dead, then a busy hospital might be the way to try it. He held on to that reminder for Della, as well. She wasn't necessarily safe here, and while that alone caused him concern, his worries about her had skyrocketed now that he knew about the baby.

Della and he made their way through the ER waiting area and toward the receptionist's desk, but before they reached it, Barrett saw Dr. Tipton coming out of an examining room.

"Alice is in there with Deputy Glenn Spence," the doctor told Barrett. "I had to give her something to calm her down."

Great. That meant Barrett might not be able to question her after all if the *calming down* zoned her out. But he could certainly talk to Dr. Tipton. Since there were several people in the waiting area, Barrett motioned for the doctor to follow him to the hall. Not exactly private space, but it would have to do. Barrett had questions about Della and the baby. Except he wasn't even sure how to get started. Della helped with that.

"Barrett knows I'm pregnant," she whispered to Dr. Tipton. "He's the baby's father."

Even with the good lead-in, Barrett still fumbled around with what to say. "I just want to make sure Della and the baby are okay," he finally managed.

Dr. Tipton didn't answer until Della gave him a nod. "They're doing as well as can be expected. I'm waiting for her lab work to come back, and as I told her, she'll need an ultrasound. If you like, I'll try to get you scheduled for that later today."

"Yes, thank you," Della said.

"You can be there for that if Della doesn't mind," the doctor offered Barrett, and then his attention drifted back to the examining room. "I'm guessing you're here to see Alice?"

"She wanted to talk to us," Barrett explained.

"So she said," Dr. Tipton verified. "She insisted, really. Let me go in and make sure she's settled down enough to have visitors," he added when he walked away from them.

Barrett hoped to hell Alice was up to it or this would be a wasted visit. For that part anyway. But not wasted on the info he'd gotten from Dr. Tipton. Della and the baby were okay. Probably.

"You don't have to come with me to the ultrasound appointment," she whispered, her voice tight and coated with an avalanche of uncertainty.

"You can't go alone," Barrett reminded her. "That's not safe."

Of course, that wasn't the same as him saying he wanted to be there for the actual appointment, but he would be. Later, Barrett would figure out how he felt about that, but he didn't need any figuring-out time to know that he had no intention of letting Della out of his sight.

"I feel as if I should say I'm sorry," she continued.

"Don't," he fired back. Not exactly a kind, gentle tone for a wounded pregnant woman, and that's why he gave himself an attitude adjustment. "We both had sex when you got pregnant. Both," he emphasized. "So, if you apologize to me, I'll just have to say it right back to you."

He'd hoped that would relieve some of the tightness on her face. It didn't. On a ragged sigh, Della leaned against the wall as if her legs were too wobbly to stand.

"I'm all right," she insisted, probably when she realized he was about to reach for her.

Barrett pulled back his hands. "Funny, you don't look all right."

She shook her head. "It's just piling up on me right now. I'd barely had time to come to terms with this pregnancy, and then we were thrown together on this murder investigation. One where your mother is a suspect. Then, we were attacked, and I was shot." Della paused, her breath shuddering. "And tomorrow is the second anniversary of Francine's murder."

Barrett knew he would have remembered that sooner or later. Knew, too, that her friend's murder had to be adding to the flashbacks Della was no doubt experiencing. There was no good time to grieve a death of a loved one, but Della was right—this was all piling on her. And the timing certainly sucked.

He couldn't think of anything to say to give her any comfort, but he reached out again. This time, he did pull her into his arms. She went stiff, likely questioning if this was a good idea. It wasn't. But she finally let go of her breath and sagged against him. He doubted she would actually cry, but he could almost feel the tears threatening.

Mindful of her gunshot wound, Barrett eased her closer, and he got an instant reminder of when they'd been lovers. The heat came despite everything else. However, it was mixed with something much stronger. This overwhelming need to protect her and the baby she carried. Since she was a cop, Della wouldn't care much for his feeling that way, but he couldn't stop himself.

Mercy, what was he going to do?

Barrett didn't have time to dwell on that, though, because Dr. Tipton came back into the hall. This time Della and he didn't jolt away from each other. Barrett simply stepped back, hoping that her legs were steadier than they seemed.

"Alice still wants to see you," the doctor said, shaking his head, "but I'm warning you not to upset her. She's right on the edge right now, and along with her panic, she's still dealing with the pain from her head injury."

Barrett and Della gave Dr. Tipton nods of reassurance that they wouldn't upset her, but Barrett had no idea if they could manage that. They likely weren't going to have a pleasant conversation with the woman.

When they stepped inside the examining room, Barrett saw Alice on the table, much as she had been the night before, after the attack. Deputy Glenn Spence was there, too, seated in the corner and looking at something on his phone, but the lanky lawman stood and walked over when he saw them.

"I've got a problem," Spence immediately said. "Lorraine Witt was attacked a few minutes ago. Someone ran her off the road."

Barrett felt the punch of surprise, followed by enough skepticism to cause that punch to fade fast. "You're sure she didn't fake it?" Barrett asked.

Spence lifted his shoulder. "Jace said it looks real enough. There are tire marks before the point of impact, and she ended up in a ditch," the deputy added. "She said two men in a black SUV did it."

Barrett muttered some profanity under his breath. He figured it'd gotten around about the men who'd attacked Della and him, and Lorraine could be using that to make herself look innocent.

"If the attack was real and these were the same thugs who shot Della, they would have tried to shoot Lorraine," Barrett pointed out.

The deputy nodded. "According to her, they did. She said she saw them point guns at her, but she had a gun, too. She aimed hers right back at them and they sped away."

"I don't suppose there were any witnesses?" Della asked.

"Nope. It happened on a remote stretch of the road between here and Culver Crossing."

Most of that road qualified as a "remote stretch" so that didn't surprise Barrett. "Was Lorraine hurt?"

"She says her shoulder's hurting, and there are some cuts on her face from where the airbags deployed. An ambulance is bringing her here because it's closer than the Culver City hospital. Plus, if it's something serious, they're better able to cope with it here."

That was true. Mercy Ridge was a much bigger hospital. Still, Barrett didn't like the idea of two of his suspects being so close to Della.

"If Jace is dealing with Lorraine's attack and

you're here with Alice," Della said, "then we're short-staffed in the office."

"We are indeed," Spence verified. "But Jace insisted you not come into work. He's put you on a mandatory leave of absence since you're hurt."

That was standard procedure, but Barrett knew it was hard to pull two deputies out of rotation. Plus, both Jace and he were facing a firestorm—especially if this latest attack was the real deal.

"Jace wanted to know if you could put Alice in the protective custody of one of your deputies," Spence went on. "Or maybe work it out so that Della and Alice are together, protected by just one lawman. It won't be for long," he added. "A day at most."

Well, hell. Spence maybe didn't know the depth of the rift between Alice and him. Or maybe he did, and it didn't matter. Cops landed between rocks and hard places all the time, and Barrett knew that's where he was right now.

"I'll work something out," he assured the deputy, and when Spence stepped to the side, Barrett went closer to the examining table.

Alice looked even more ashen than she had the night before. No fresh tears, though. Instead, there was a shell-shocked expression that seemed to be bone-deep. He wanted to be immune to that look, to her weary eyes that she lifted to meet his. But he was human, and this was a woman on the brink of a very bad place.

"I remember," Alice said, her voice as drained as the rest of her.

She already had his attention, but that caused Della to move to the other side of the examining table. "Remember what?" Della asked.

Alice's eyelids fluttered down, and she shook her head. Now the tears came. "Everything."

Chapter Nine

Della hadn't thought anything could take her mind off Barrett learning about the pregnancy, but she'd obviously been wrong. Every muscle in her body tensed and she held her breath because she was afraid that Alice was about to make a confession.

Of murder.

"I'm listening," Barrett said, and it seemed to Della that he was also holding his breath.

"I remember that man who kidnapped me," Alice explained. She shook her head. "I was unconscious, but I came to when he was dragging me into the woods. I saw his face."

Barrett took out his phone, pulled up LeBeau's picture from the investigation file and showed it to Alice. "Was it this man?"

"Yes," she answered without hesitation. "He wasn't alone. I didn't see who was with him, but he was calling out to someone. He said something like *Hold your horses, I'll be right there after I take care of the woman*."

"*Take care of the woman*," Della muttered, and she wanted to cringe. Because that sounded as if he'd had intentions of killing her. Of course, maybe he'd just meant to set her up, but even if that had been the plan, Alice could have still been killed by the blow to the head.

"Did you hear this other person speak?" Barrett asked.

"Yes." Again, Alice didn't hesitate. "It was another man. Not Robert, though," she quickly added. "And I couldn't make out what he said. But I heard a sound." Alice shuddered and clamped her teeth over her bottom lip for a few seconds. "It was the sound a person makes when they're in great pain. I think that's when this person killed Robert, and I believe Robert was the one in pain."

Barrett stayed silent a moment, no doubt processing all of that. "You didn't kill Casto?" he pressed.

"No." Alice looked him straight in the eyes when she said that. "I didn't kill anyone."

Della certainly believed her, and she thought Barrett did, too. Plus, what Alice was saying meshed with the evidence. Maybe it would mesh even more if the fingerprints on the murder weapon didn't belong to Alice and the CSIs found proof that someone other than LeBeau, Casto and Alice was in the woods last night. The last one wouldn't be much of a stretch since the two shooters had clearly been in the area because they'd attacked Barrett and her near there.

"There's no need for Alice to stay here," Dr. Tipton said, breaking the silence in the room.

Barrett nodded, adding a soft groan, and he looked at the deputy. "Why don't you help us get Alice to my cruiser?" In other words, keep watch when they were outside in case those gunmen were out there. "I'll take Della and her to my place, and you can get back to Culver Crossing."

Spence blew out what sounded like a breath of relief. No doubt because he was feeling pressed to get back to work. Della was feeling that same pressure. Jace was a good boss, and she hated that he was shorthanded. Still, Della was feeling an even greater need to make sure her baby stayed safe. It'd be harder to manage that if she returned to the job.

Spence helped Alice off the table, and after she signed some papers for the doctor, they went out through the waiting room and to the exit. Barrett and Spence looked out, checking the parking lot, and they must not have seen anything alarming because they then hurried Alice into the back seat of the cruiser. Della sat shotgun, and the moment Barrett, Alice and she had latched their seat belts, Barrett sped off.

Della hadn't realized she was holding her breath until her chest started to ache, and it twisted at her that just being outside brought on the overwhelming fear. There'd been plenty of times as a cop that she was afraid, but this was many steps past that now, because if something happened to her, it also happened to the baby.

Keeping watch around them, Barrett drove through town and toward his ranch. Della kept watch, too, not just on their surroundings but also on Alice and Barrett. She caught him glancing at her stomach and figured he was giving plenty of thought to the baby. There was no way for him to put something like that out of his mind, but it wasn't good for them to lose focus like this.

"Thank you," Alice said from the back seat. "I know you don't want me to be in your home."

"No," Barrett said, and almost immediately he tacked on some muttered profanity to that blunt admission. "It won't be for long," he added, his tone just a tad softer.

Della wanted to say that she knew how hard this would be for Barrett to have Alice under his roof. Especially since she'd be right there with them. He had so much on his plate right now. Heck, so did she. But despite that full plate, they were going to have to talk about the baby. Maybe by the time they got around to doing that, he would have figured out some things. Maybe she would, too.

Thankfully, there was no other traffic on the road, which helped Della's nerves. Also thankfully, an SUV would stand out here, where most folks drove pickups. Of course, the cruiser would stand out as well, but she hoped that would be in a good way. The gunman had attacked them while they'd been in Barrett's truck—which hadn't been bullet resistant. Attacking them in a cruiser wouldn't be a smart move. Though depending on how much these guys wanted Barrett and her dead, they could still go for it.

Della breathed a little easier when Barrett pulled to a stop in front of his ranch. She doubted that Alice was feeling an easiness, though. The woman looked at the pastures, the barns and the house. A house that'd once belonged to her in-laws, Barrett's paternal grandparents. After Barrett's father had committed suicide, his grandfather had moved into the main house so he could help out with Barrett and his brothers.

"A long time," Alice whispered.

Yes. Over two decades. Still, those memories had to feel fresh to her. At least they wouldn't be staying in the main house that'd once been Alice's home. Leo now lived there with his two-year-old daughter, and Della figured Barrett wouldn't be taking Alice anywhere near there.

Ignoring Alice's comment, Barrett went into cop mode and hurried them all inside, where he immediately locked the door and checked the security system. It was still armed, but he went to all the windows and doors to check for any signs of a break-in.

"I'm sorry about having to come here," Alice whispered to Della. "I mean, I'm sorry to interrupt anything Barrett and you have to do." Her eyes widened, and she blushed. "I didn't mean it like *that*. I know you said Barrett and you weren't back together, but I meant the investigation. You two probably have plenty to say to each other."

Yes, they did. And only a portion of that applied to the investigation.

Barrett came back out of the hall, and he snared Alice's gaze. "You can use my room. The master bedroom," he clarified. "Della's in the guest room, and I can sleep on the pullout sofa in my office."

Alice was shaking her head before he even finished. "I'm not taking your room. The pullout is fine." And as if to prove that, she headed in that direction, issuing another apology.

Barrett muttered some more profanity, and he lifted his eyes to the ceiling as if asking for some divine help. If it came, Della would certainly welcome it.

"Don't you apologize again," Barrett warned Della when she opened her mouth. But he winced and waved that off. "I haven't worked it all out in my head yet, but then I figure neither have you."

He was right about that. "The only thing I'm certain of right now is that I want this baby, and I need to keep him or her safe."

"Him or her," he repeated, and judging from his expression, those pronouns made it very real to him. A boy or a girl. Their son or their daughter. "Yeah, I want the baby safe, too, and that's why we have to declare a truce. For now, let's take our past relationship off the table and concentrate on finding a killer."

That sounded, well, good. "Is it doable? I mean, us declaring a truce?" Della asked.

The corner of his mouth lifted in that half smile. The one that had always sent her heart and body zinging. It was still plenty effective because that's what happened to her now.

And Barrett noticed.

He shook his head, mumbled something that Della didn't catch and then surprised Della by walking over to her. She'd have thought he'd keep his distance from her. As far as he could get. Instead, he slipped his arm around her and eased her to him. Not too close, though. This was obviously a hug of comfort, and Della very much needed it. She wasn't alone in this ordeal, although sometimes it felt like it. But not when Barrett was holding her.

"Be honest with me," he said. "How much are you hurting right now?"

"At the moment, not much at all." Della winced when she heard her tone. It was breath and silk. The tone of an aroused woman.

He looked down at her, the corner of his mouth kicking up again, and his gaze met hers. Maybe there was arousal in his eyes as well, but there also seemed to be some resignation.

So much for them putting their past on the back burner.

Their past was suddenly right in front of them, and Della felt the heat slide through her. Unfortunately, Barrett felt it, too. She knew that because of the way his grip tightened on her, and he kept his gaze fastened to her face. Specifically, to her mouth.

"I'm going to regret this," he muttered a split second before he kissed her.

And there it was. No slide of heat this time but a full slam of fire. It was as if no time had passed between them. As if they weren't neck-deep in a serious investigation that could get them killed. All of that vanished, and all that Della could think about—and feel—was his mouth on hers.

Barrett obviously hadn't lost any of his kissing skills in the past two months. He claimed her, using his tightened grip to pull her even closer. Until they were pressed together with his chest against her breasts. That upped the heat even more, and the urgency came, her body instantly wanting more.

That was the trouble with them being past lovers. Lovers who'd had great sex too many times to count. A lone kiss could feel like hours of foreplay and could make the need for each other seem urgent and primal.

Della was certainly feeling both right now.

It was somewhat of a miracle that Barrett's kiss could make her forget the pain, their messy situation and everything else other than the taste of him. The feel of him against her mouth. She wanted to sink right in, to feed the heat, to lead him straight to his bed.

But that shouldn't happen.

Della mentally repeated that to herself, but it took a triple reminder for her to finally pull her mouth from his. Even then the need continued to soar, fueled now by the fact that she was looking at his amazing face. Yes, Barrett had always hit the higher rung on the attraction ladder.

"I told you I was going to regret it," he said.

But she didn't see much regret in him. Like her, his breathing was uneven, and she could feel his heartbeat thudding against her chest. Della was certain her own heart was doing some thudding. Along with breaking a little.

"Life has a twisted sense of humor," she told him, and she stepped back. "I ended things with you so I could get on with my life. So I could have the home and kids I'd always wanted. Ironic that I'll have the child, but everything else is a mess."

He made a sound of agreement, but Barrett didn't get to voice it because his phone rang, and when Daniel's name popped up on the screen, he answered it right away. He also put the call on speaker.

"Is Alice really at your place?" his brother asked the moment he was on the line.

"Yeah." Barrett's jaw was tight with that response. "By the way, you're on speaker, and Della's here."

"I figured as much. How'd it happen that you took Alice there?"

Barrett took a deep breath. "It seemed the reasonable thing to do since both Della and she are in danger."

Daniel made his own sound, and Della thought she heard his underlying sentiment. For Daniel and the rest of the Logans, there was nothing reasonable when it came to their mother.

"I was about to call a marshal friend and see if they can arrange a safe house," Barrett explained. "For Alice," he added. "Maybe for Della, too, if I can convince her to go."

"Good luck with that," Daniel grumbled.

Under normal circumstances, no way would Della have even considered being tucked away at a safe house. She was a cop and didn't need such protection. But there was the baby. Which meant she had to at least consider it.

"I've been plowing through the financial records on Lorraine and Curran," Daniel went on a moment later. "Nothing so far is standing out for Lorraine, but I'm having Scottie do a lot more digging there. But Curran's a different story. I found something that really stands out."

Della automatically moved closer to the phone. "What?" Barrett and she asked in unison.

"I figured that'd get your attention. It certainly got mine. Listen to this—over the past six months, Curran has made multiple payments to a private investigator. Rory Silva."

Hearing the name felt like a punch to Della, and she shook her head. "Rory Silva?" she repeated. "As in Francine's brother?"

"Yep," Daniel verified. "I'm guessing you didn't know he'd done some work for Curran?"

"No." Della shoved her hair from her face. "I knew he was a PI, of course." She also knew that Francine and Rory hadn't always gotten along. In fact, they'd argued over their grandparents' inheritance for years.

An argument that'd ended when Francine had been murdered.

Della wanted to force any thoughts of that aside. Rory hadn't killed Francine. He'd had a solid alibi and had been broken up over his sister's death. At least he had seemed broken up. Now she had to wonder why Rory had gone to work for a man who had known criminal ties.

"There's more," Daniel went on. "While I was trying to figure out the financials, I got a call from San Antonio PD. They've been going through LeBeau's place, and they found his phone. Not the burner cell he had on him but rather one he used often. I guess he didn't want to carry it with him while committing multiple felonies."

"Please tell me LeBeau called the person who hired him to kidnap Alice," Barrett said.

"Well, he didn't call Curran," Daniel added. "But he did call Rory. Many, many times. Judging from the frequency and length of the calls, I have to say that Rory and our dead guy were friends."

Chapter Ten

"Rory," Barrett repeated. Then, he cursed. Because this was a connection to the investigation that he definitely didn't like.

Barrett knew Rory, of course. Heck, he'd even talked with the man on several occasions so he could maybe find a new angle for Francine's murder investigation. But Barrett hadn't seen or spoken to him in over a year.

That would change.

"Call Rory and have him come in for an interview," Barrett instructed Daniel. "Don't make it a request. Make it an order, and I want him in ASAP."

"I want to see him, too," Della insisted.

Barrett had known she'd need to be in on something like that, but it gave him a dilemma of sorts. He couldn't leave Alice here alone at his place and didn't especially want to tie up one of his deputies with bodyguard duty. Still, he'd have to do just that, because he didn't want to take Alice outside until moving her to a safe house. It was bad enough that Della would be on the road where those gunmen could try to come after her again.

"I'll get Rory in here right away," Daniel assured him, and he ended the call.

Barrett stood there a moment, working out what this connection between Curran and Rory could possibly mean. Judging from the way Della's forehead was bunched up, she was doing the same thing.

"How well do you know Rory?" Barrett asked her.

"Apparently not well enough." She stayed silent a moment longer. "Francine never mentioned that he had any shady associations. I would have remembered that. But Francine and Rory didn't get along, so it's possible he would have kept something like this from her."

"It's also possible that Rory didn't have those shady connections when his sister was still alive," Barrett reminded her. "Or Rory hid them."

It would have been stupid for Rory to announce to his cop sister that he might be skirting along the edges of the law. Or outright breaking it.

Della made a sound of agreement. "You'll question Curran about this, too," she said.

"Oh, yeah." Barrett turned and went to the table where he'd left his laptop. Good thing, because now he wouldn't have to go into his office—where Alice was—to get it. "I want to check for any lab reports and then do a check on Rory. Then, I can call a reserve deputy to come out here and stay with Alice while you and I go back in."

"If you want to go ahead and make that call, I can start the check on Rory," she offered.

Barrett nodded. Right now, he'd take all the help he could get, and Della was a good cop. She'd be able to do that as fast as he could.

While she booted up his laptop, Barrett considered his options, and he settled on calling in Buddy Adler, who lived just up the road. It would mean dipping into the sheriff's department budget to bring Buddy on board and Barrett might get some flak over that, but this way he wouldn't be pulling his regular deputies away from the mountain of work they were facing because of this double murder investigation.

Before Barrett could call Buddy, however, his phone dinged with a text message from Daniel.

Rory's on his way in. He'll be here in under an hour.

Good. Barrett responded:

Arrange to have Curran back in, too. I want to see him after I've talked to Rory.

Thankfully, Buddy answered Barrett's call right away, and he agreed to come over immediately. Which was good. Until he looked at Della's face. Without the flush of arousal, she just looked tired.

"I can have you watch the interviews from here," Barrett offered. "I can rig it so you can do that on my laptop. You'd even be able to ask Rory questions."

Della shook her head. "I'm going with you."

He'd figured that would be her response, but he had to try. Barrett nearly pressed her to stay and get some rest. He might have won an argument about it if he pointed out that this kind of fatigue wasn't good for the baby. But even if she stayed put, rest likely wouldn't happen. Like him, she was probably revved with the prospect that they might get answers.

"I'll check on Alice," she offered. "And I'll let her know that Buddy will be watching her. She knows him, right?"

"Yes, she does." Something that Barrett hadn't actually remembered. But Buddy had been working for Barrett's family for the past thirty years. The hand would have definitely been around during Alice's departure. And his father's suicide. That might not make it easy for Alice to see Buddy, but at the moment Barrett couldn't worry about her discomfort.

While Della was with Alice, Barrett went to his laptop to check the lab reports. What he read there had him frowning. The smeared prints on the knife were still inconclusive, and at this point it might stay that way. The lab techs couldn't identify something that wasn't there.

He moved on to the financials next and saw that Daniel had made good progress. Curran had paid Rory a total of nearly eight grand. Not a fortune exactly, but it indicated that Rory had worked plenty of hours for Curran. But doing what exactly? That was something Barrett intended to find out.

The next report showed that San Antonio PD had made progress, too, with LeBeau's cell phone records. Rory and LeBeau had talked at least twenty times over the past three months. Some of the conversations had lasted nearly a half hour. Coupled with the fact that there were no business payments from LeBeau to Rory, Barrett believed Daniel had it right.

LeBeau and Rory were friends.

And while there was no crime in that, it did mean Rory had a connection to a killer. That in turn meant Rory was connected to the current investigation.

Hell.

Barrett hoped this didn't circle back around to

Francine's murder. Della had enough to handle without adding a dose of the past.

He heard the sound of an approaching vehicle and automatically drew his weapon. But as expected, it was Buddy. Barrett disarmed the security system to let the man in.

"Thanks for coming so fast," Barrett said just as Della came back into the room. Buddy tipped his Stetson in greeting before he took it off and hung it on the peg next to the door.

"Alice knows you'll be here," Della explained to Buddy. "She said she'd be sleeping while we're gone, that she's exhausted."

The exhaustion part was likely true, but it could be that Alice just wanted to avoid someone who'd been so close to her late husband. Della wasn't the only one who had enough emotional stuff to deal with.

Della and Barrett gathered their things, and Barrett gave Buddy instructions on how to arm the security system after they were gone. Buddy also wouldn't hesitate to call for backup if needed. In a pinch, he could also alert the other hands who'd be working both Daniel's and Leo's ranches.

There was plenty of open pasture around his house, something that Barrett was thankful for because he was able to check out their surroundings and make sure a gunman wasn't lying in wait. There wasn't. But both Della and he stayed on alert during the drive to his office.

As he'd done on their previous trip, Barrett parked the cruiser right in front, and Della and he hurried inside. He'd thought he would continue to go over the financials and reports, but he instantly spotted Rory, who was pacing in front of Barrett's office door.

"He just got here," Daniel told them in a low voice. "And I'm not sure if he's nervous or if that's the way he usually is."

"Nervous," Della supplied.

She didn't get a chance to add more because Rory spotted them and made a beeline for them. He looked young, younger than Francine had been at the time of her death, and he was wearing jeans and a button-up blue shirt. His black hair fell nearly to his shoulders.

Rory reached out as if he might hug her, but he seemed to change his mind when his attention landed on her bandaged arm. "You're hurt," he said. "I'd heard you were, but I hoped I heard wrong."

"It's not bad," Della assured him. "You remember Sheriff Logan," she added, tipping her head toward Barrett.

"Of course." Rory shook Barrett's hand. The guy's palm was sweaty, proving that Della had been right about the nervous part. Of course,

Rory had been summoned to a police station on the heels of a murder.

The murder of someone he knew.

Rory was a fool if he hadn't thought he'd be questioned. Then again, maybe he hadn't believed the cops would make a connection between LeBeau, Curran and him.

"Thank you for coming so fast, Rory," Della said, and she looked up at Barrett. "Should we go ahead and take this into interview?"

Barrett nodded, but he let Della lead the way. A good call, he thought, because Rory fell in step alongside her, and the look he gave Della appeared to be a friendly one.

"I'd intended to call you," Rory told her as they walked. "I mean because of the anniversary of Francine's death. I didn't figure you had anything new to tell me, but I thought it was a good time to touch base."

"I'm still investigating it," Della answered, but there was something in her tone. Something with an edge of a threat.

Barrett knew that Rory had never been a top suspect for his sister's murder, but Francine and he had bickered over family money, so that meant Barrett had never removed the man as a possibility. He'd thought that Della had done just that—eliminated Rory. But maybe not.

They went into the interview room, and Barrett closed the door and set up the recorder. Rory stayed silent until Della started reading him his rights.

"Wait a minute." Rory got out of the chair where he'd just sat. "You're arresting me? For what?" His tone and expression certainly weren't so friendly now, and he volleyed hard looks at both of them.

"It's procedure," Della assured him. "That way if something comes up during the interview, all bases are covered." She finished Mirandizing him. "Would you like to have an attorney here with you?" she asked.

Rory stayed quiet a moment, giving that some thought. "No. Not at this exact moment." His jaw was tight now, and he paused again. "This is about Harris LeBeau's murder?"

So, he had heard about it. Barrett would have been shocked if he hadn't. He nodded, sat. So did Rory and Della.

"Can you tell me where you were between six last night and one this morning?" Barrett started.

"Home," Rory readily answered, but then he cursed. "Alone. In other words, I don't have an alibi. I didn't know I'd need one. But I didn't kill LeBeau. He was my friend."

Good. That was one thing he needed verified. "Close friend?" Barrett pressed.

Rory shrugged. "Not really. He had a lot of contacts that helped with some of my PI jobs, and every now and then we'd meet for a drink."

"LeBeau had a criminal record," Della pointed out. "Were you aware of that?"

"Sure. He talked about getting caught with stolen goods. But I also ran him and knew that he'd been arrested for assault." Rory sighed. "He didn't exactly take responsibility for what he'd done. He claimed he'd gotten mixed up with the wrong crowd, but it'd been four years since his last arrest."

Barrett mulled that over a moment. "So, you used LeBeau as a criminal informant?" he asked.

Another shrug. "Sometimes. But I swear I thought he was clean." His gaze met Barrett's. "But you're going to tell me he was into something bad, and that it got him killed."

Oh, yeah. Whatever LeBeau had been hired to do, it'd likely gotten him killed, but Barrett kept that to himself. "When's the last time you saw LeBeau?"

"About a week ago. And no, he didn't mention that he was about to go off the deep end and do something stupid." Rory leaned forward, resting his forearms on the metal table. "I heard he was there last night when another guy was killed. Robert Casto. Is that true?"

"LeBeau was there," Barrett verified. "Any idea why?"

"None," Rory quickly answered, and he huffed, shook his head. "I'm sorry, but I just don't know anything about it." He went stiff and turned to Della. "Do you think any of what happened has something to do with Francine's murder?"

"We're looking into that," she said. Which was a way of telling Rory pretty much nothing, because they were looking into plenty of things right now.

"Tell me about Wilbur Curran," Barrett threw out there, and because he was carefully watching Rory's expression, he saw the flash of surprise in the man's eyes.

"Uh, I've done some PI work for him," Rory answered, but this time it wasn't fast, and hesitation replaced the surprise.

"Why'd Curran hire you?" Barrett pressed when Rory didn't volunteer anything else.

Rory groaned, shook his head. "I can't discuss Curran with you."

Barrett stared at him. "This is a murder investigation, and you're not a lawyer. You don't have client-attorney privilege." Though Rory could argue that he did have an obligation to keep his clients' business under wraps, and that's why Barrett offered Rory a compromise. "Just give me the broad strokes. I'm not looking for specifics." Not at the moment anyway. But Barrett would if he sensed anything was off here.

Rory glanced at Della, maybe hoping that she would give him an out. The only thing she gave him was a stern cop's expression. Rory finally sighed and shifted his attention back to Barrett.

"Curran wanted me to look into any charges that you might file against him in the money laundering investigation," Rory explained. "He believes you'll continue the investigation against him."

"I will," Barrett assured him. And he gave that some thought. It wasn't a surprise that Curran would hire someone to poke into any possible evidence or links that could be used against him, but he had to wonder how far Curran expected the PI to go. "Did Curran ask you to bend the law in any way?"

Rory's eyes widened. "No." And he repeated his denial while he shook his head. "Curran didn't ask, and I wouldn't have done it even if that's what he'd wanted. I need to keep my PI's license. It's how I make my living."

Maybe Rory was telling the truth, but Barrett would dig deeper to see if anything was there. For now, though, he went with a different angle.

"Because of your connection to LeBeau," Barrett went on, "I can get access to some of your records. I can and will also talk to any of LeBeau's associates about him…and you. Tell me, Rory, am I going to find out anything that'll make me think you're hiding something or that you aren't being completely honest with me?"

The muscles in Rory's jaw went to war with each other, and he looked away, causing Barrett to groan. There was something.

"Spill it," Barrett demanded.

Rory squeezed his eyes shut a moment. "I have debts," he finally said. "Lots of them, and I'm in danger of losing my house. Losing everything," he added in a hoarse mumble.

"What happened to Francine's life insurance money?" Della immediately asked him. "That was a five-hundred-thousand-dollar policy."

Rory appeared to try to steel himself up when he turned to her. "It's gone. All gone. I used it to pay off gambling debts, but it wasn't enough. I still owe the wrong people a lot of money."

In other words, loan sharks where the interest would just keep piling up. And since not paying them off could result in bodily harm or worse, that made Rory a desperate man. One who might indeed skirt the law for a client who'd help him get the sharks off his back.

"You're sure you didn't do anything for Curran or LeBeau that'd give you the cash you need?" Barrett pressed.

"I'm sure." This time Rory looked him in the eyes when he answered.

Barrett took a moment to consider everything he'd just heard, and he would have asked a few more questions if there hadn't been a knock at the door. It was Daniel, and he motioned for Barrett to step into the hall with him. He did, and Della joined them a moment later.

Daniel handed him a piece of paper. "This just came in from the lab, and I figured you'd want to read it."

Barrett did exactly that. So did Della. She moved next to him, her uninjured arm sliding against his. Several words practically jumped right out at Barrett.

Alice Logan. Fingerprints. Planted.

"The lab guy said the pressure points aren't right on the handle of the knife used to murder Casto," Daniel summarized for them. "The prints belong to Alice all right, but it's their conclusion that someone held her hand on the knife and planted them there."

The long breath that Della blew out was definitely one of relief. Barrett supposed he should be relieved, too, to have one less murder suspect, but this led him to a critical question.

Who had set up Alice and why?

Probably not LeBeau. No, this likely led back to the person who'd hired LeBeau and those other thugs who'd shot at Della and him. He doubted Rory had been the one to do that, but it was possible the loan sharks—or Curran—had pressured him into putting together something like this.

Barrett handed the report to Daniel, and he was about to go back in to interview when Della's phone buzzed. Since they were still arm to arm, Barrett had no trouble seeing Dr. Tipton's name on the screen.

"I need to take this," Della said, stepping away from them.

Barrett didn't follow her, mainly because that would have made Daniel suspicious. Or rather more suspicious than he already was. His brothers were definitely picking up on the vibe between Della and him, but Barrett seriously doubted that they'd figured out Della was carrying his child.

"You want me to finish up with Rory?" Daniel asked, eyeing Della, who was now having a whispered conversation with the doctor. "I was listening to the interview while I was working so I can pick up where you left off."

Barrett hated to dump this on Daniel, but there was no way he could concentrate until he knew what was going on with Della. He didn't care much for the way he saw her shoulders tense.

"Thanks. I'd appreciate you doing that," Barrett told Daniel, and his brother gave them both one last glance before he went into the room with Rory.

Thankfully, Barrett didn't have to wait long. It was only a couple of seconds longer before Della ended the call. However, when she turned toward him, he got confirmation that something was wrong.

"What happened?" Barrett asked.

"Dr. Tipton wants me at the hospital right now," Della said, her voice shaky. "There are some problems with my lab tests."

Chapter Eleven

Della tried to tamp down her racing heartbeat and breathing. She also tried not to go into panic mode. But it was hard to do because this wasn't just about her.

This could be about the baby.

"Did Dr. Tipton say specifically what was wrong?" Barrett whispered to her as they made their way to the front of the building. It sounded as if he was trying not to panic as well, but his voice was louder and stronger when he told the dispatcher that he had to head out for a meeting.

"No," Della answered once they were out of earshot of the dispatchers and deputies in the bullpen. "He didn't want to get into it all over the phone. Plus, he wants to go ahead and do the ultrasound."

Della considered all the possibilities. Then, pushed those possibilities aside. Just going out into the open could be dangerous, and she didn't want to add to their troubles by being reckless.

She kept watch around them as Barrett and she hurried out and into the cruiser.

Problems with lab tests, Della mentally repeated. Well, she knew it wasn't the actual pregnancy test because the doctor hadn't gotten back those results the night before. This had to be something else.

Even though the hospital wasn't far, it seemed to take an eternity for them to get there. Barrett parked by the ER, and they hurried in, making a beeline up the hall to Dr. Tipton's office. Just as the doctor had said, he was waiting for them and ushered them right in.

"What's wrong?" Della immediately demanded, not wanting to wait for polite greetings.

"It's not that bad," he assured her, and seemed alarmed. Probably because she looked ready to come unglued. "But you're anemic, and your blood sugar's a little higher than I'd like."

"Is that serious?" Barrett said at the same moment that Della asked, "What does that mean?"

"Well, the anemia is a fairly easy fix with supplements I can prescribe. The blood sugar, though, will require some monitoring. We don't want it to get out of control because it can cause complications with the pregnancy and the baby."

Oh, mercy. That definitely wasn't good.

"Your OB will give you this information

sheet." Dr. Tipton handed her some papers he took from his desk and motioned for them to follow him out of the office and back down the hall. "But I wanted you to go ahead and have it. For now, your OB will likely want to monitor you more closely."

It was a reminder that she needed to make the OB appointment ASAP. Yes, she had a boatload of stuff going on, but the baby had to be her top priority.

"I managed to squeeze you in for an ultrasound appointment," Dr. Tipton continued, leading them into another room. "After the blood loss and shock you just went through, I wanted to go ahead and get it done. I can have the results sent to your OB. Is your OB here in Mercy Ridge?"

"No, Culver Crossing. Dr. Abernathy. I haven't actually had an appointment with him yet, but he was someone my doctor recommended."

Della had been reading through the info he'd given her, but the moment they stepped inside, she saw the tech was already there, waiting for them.

"I'll need you to take off your holster, lift your top and lower your jeans," the tech said. According to her name tag, she was Amanda

Pierce. Amanda then looked at Barrett. "Will you be staying for this?"

"Yes," Barrett answered after glancing at Della.

Della didn't exactly give him the green light, but she was a little surprised that he wanted to be part of this. She doubted he'd resolved all of his doubts about fatherhood. However, maybe his worries for the baby were as sky-high as hers.

It was obvious the tech was in a hurry because she didn't waste any time helping Della onto the exam table. Helping her, too, lift her top and push down the waist of her jeans. Of course, that meant she was showing a lot of skin, including her flimsy black lace bra. Even though Barrett had seen every inch of her naked, it was unnerving now.

The tech smeared some goop on her belly and began to move the ultrasound probe over Della. Immediately, some images appeared on the screen. Exactly what images, Della didn't know. To her it looked like a snowstorm surrounding a small blob. Then she realized that was the baby.

The baby, she mentally repeated, the emotions going through her like a freight train. Della certainly hadn't expected to feel this much, this fast at merely seeing her child, but she did.

She glanced at Barrett to see how he was re-acting. He, too, was riveted to the screen, and she didn't think it was her imagination that he looked a little unsteady.

"It appears you're a little further along than you thought," Dr. Tipton said. "I'm estimating closer to three months rather than two."

So, she hadn't gotten pregnant right before she'd ended things with Barrett after all. She wasn't sure why she found that, well, comfort-ing, but she did. She doubted, though, that Bar-rett was feeling much comfort about it. After all, she was still pregnant, and he was still going to be a father.

"We can't tell the sex of the baby just yet," the doctor went on. "Probably by next month, though."

Next month. Not long at all. Then she'd know if she was going to have a son or a daughter. It didn't matter to her. But what did matter was that everything was okay.

"Do you see anything wrong?" Della man-aged to ask.

Dr. Tipton looked over his shoulder at her and gave her a reassuring smile. "All looks well. Of course, like I said, your OB will want to see this."

The relief came, and it was just as swift and strong as her emotions at seeing the baby. Her child hadn't been hurt because of the shooting and blood loss. Everything was okay. For now. Della had to make sure it stayed that way.

The tech finished, and after she'd cleaned off the goop, she helped Della off the table so she could fix her clothes. While Della did that, Barrett asked Dr. Tipton about the high blood sugar issue, and she listened to their conversation while volleying glances at the images of the baby that were still on the screen.

"My advice is for you to make sure Della gets lots of rest," Dr. Tipton explained to Barrett. "And stop by the pharmacy and pick up those supplements."

The pharmacy wasn't part of the hospital but rather up the street, and Della could immediately see Barrett's hesitation about her going there. "Any chance someone else can pick them up for her?" Barrett asked.

The doctor obviously heard the concern in Barrett's voice and saw it on Della's face. "Sure. I'll call them to make sure they know what's going on. Remember to make that OB appointment," he added as Barrett and she made their way out.

"I'm taking you back to the ranch so you can lie down," Barrett informed her. "You can call the OB on the way."

Normally, she would have bristled at him taking charge like this. At anyone taking charge, she mentally amended. But the truth was, she was exhausted. And it would do both her and the baby some good if she could rest. Of course, for that to happen, she'd have to turn off her mind, something that Della doubted was going to happen. Yes, the baby was at the forefront but so was the investigation. They had to solve this case for them to find any kind of normalcy.

"I'll be able to tell Alice about the prints on the knife," Della said after they were in the cruiser.

Barrett glanced at her as if surprised by the topic she'd chosen. After all, they had plenty else to discuss, including what had just gone on in the hospital. "I'll do that. I meant it when I said you were going to get some sleep. I don't want you reading reports or doing anything else with this investigation."

His offer to tell Alice was huge since Della knew he wanted to avoid any contact with his mother. "I'll have to tell Jace soon," she went on several moments later as Barrett drove through town. "Tell him I'm pregnant, I mean. He'll put me on desk duty."

That was something that definitely wouldn't have sat well with her if she'd been merely hurt. But being out in the field was too big of a risk.

"Later, after you've rested, you and I can

talk," Barrett said. Judging by his tone, he wasn't looking forward to that. Or so she thought, but then he added, "I'll be there for this baby." He kept his attention on the road as he drove out of town. "I'll be there for *you*."

It was a good thing she was sitting because that robbed her of some breath. Those were definitely words she hadn't expected Barrett to say. And maybe he didn't want to say them. He could be looking at all of this as one giant obligation, just as he had when he'd stepped up to raise his brothers after his father's suicide. His grandfather had helped with that, of course, but Barrett had done more than his fair share of parenting.

Della wanted to give him an out. She wanted to tell him that he wouldn't have to get emotionally invested the way he had with Daniel and Leo. But she was afraid that anything she said right now would just hit some very raw nerves. It was best that she give him some time. As much time as they could manage, anyway, considering that in about six months they'd be parents.

"Hell," Barrett muttered, getting her complete attention when he drew his gun.

Della automatically did the same, and just ahead on the road, she spotted the black SUV. She couldn't be sure it was the same one their attackers had used, but she took out her phone to call in the plates. She wanted an ID on whoever owned the vehicle.

Trying to tamp down the surge of adrenaline, she looked down at her phone. However, she didn't manage to press a number because Barrett cursed again, and he jerked the steering wheel hard to the right. Della got just a glimpse of something in the road. A small black box.

And the blast roared through the cruiser.

BARRETT DIDN'T HAVE time to react other than slamming on his brakes. That might have saved Della and him, though, because instead of being directly on top of the explosive device when it went off, they were still a few yards away from it.

That was bad enough, though.

The front end of the cruiser lifted off the pavement, shaking them like rag dolls, and the airbags bashed into them. Barrett had a hard flash of fear for the baby and her, but he had to shove that out of his mind so he could assess their situation.

And brace himself in case this wasn't the end of the attack.

Beside him, Della batted back the airbag. She also moaned and winced. That caused his heart to slam in his chest, but then he realized she was holding her arm. All the jostling around had likely hurt her stitches. Hell, here she was recovering from the gunshot wound, and she might have other injuries. That reminder replaced some of the shock and fear with anger. Barrett would make sure whoever had done this would pay for it.

"Are you okay?" he asked, shoving aside his own airbag.

"I think so." She sounded dazed, but at least she was coherent. And she'd managed to hang on to her gun. So had Barrett. That was somewhat of a miracle, considering the impact. "You?"

"I'm fine." But he had no idea if that was even true. Physically, he thought he was okay, but thoughts of worst-case scenarios were flying all over the place.

Because of a thick cloud of smoke and the residue from the airbags, Barrett couldn't see much, but most of the front end of the cruiser was now a mangled heap. Thankfully, though, the damage hadn't extended into the cab of the vehicle. That was something at least.

But it might not last.

There could be a second device nearby. And worse. The person or persons who'd left that bomb or whatever it was on the road could be circling back to try to finish the job they'd started.

Barrett tried to keep watch around them and listen for any sounds of an approaching vehicle or footsteps, but he couldn't hear anything like that. He fired off a quick text to Daniel to request backup. They'd need a bomb squad, too, but Daniel could arrange for that once he was on scene. Right now, Barrett just needed help. And he needed to get Della and him moving.

"The gas in the tank could catch fire," he told her.

Della made a sharp gasp, and, still wincing, she leaned forward, no doubt trying to see the engine. There was still some smoke, hopefully not from a fire and only steam from the radiator, but Barrett couldn't risk them staying put.

Since the cruiser was already on the side of the road, it wasn't that far to the ditch, only a couple of feet, and it was on Della's side. That was both good and bad. It meant she'd be able to get out of the cruiser, but once outside she could be an easy target for gunmen. Barrett had a bad feeling that their attackers weren't just going to drive off and assume they'd done the job of killing Della and him.

Beyond the ditch was flat pasture and a fence. No trees or shrubs, which meant no place for them to take cover in case they had to shoot.

Still, it would have to do until backup could arrive.

While still keeping watch and listening, Barrett leaned over, and he opened Della's door. "I'll get out on this side. You get out on yours," he instructed. "Drop down into the ditch as fast as you can."

Despite her obvious pain, she managed to give him a flat look. "You'll be on the road, right in the possible line of fire."

"Possible," Barrett emphasized. "Right now the biggest risk is for us to be in this vehicle." Again, that could be true, but his every instinct was telling him to move—now.

"I'll get out and cover you," Della insisted. She grabbed her bag, putting it on across her body so her hands would still be free. He nearly told her to leave it behind, but it no doubt held some extra ammo and her phone. Things they might need. "Then, we can get into the ditch together."

It was playing dirty, but Barrett would do whatever it took to get her moving. "Think of the baby," was all he said.

She muttered some profanity that was no doubt aimed at him, but Della did that while getting out of the cruiser. She did just as he'd wanted and practically toppled down into the ditch where hopefully she'd have decent cover.

It wouldn't be enough, though.

He'd need to get them moving down the ditch and away from the cruiser. The need for that became even more urgent when Barrett caught the scent of something he definitely didn't want to smell.

Gasoline.

Hell. It could blow up at any second.

Keeping his gun ready, he got out, using his own door for cover for a couple of seconds while he scanned the road and pastures around them. He spotted the SUV about twenty yards ahead. Not parked there, either. The driver had the vehicle in Reverse and was coming right at them. And that wasn't all. A second man was leaning out the passenger's side window, and he had a gun aimed right at Barrett.

Barrett couldn't stay put in case this thug started shooting in the ditch. Plus, if Della heard shots, she might not stay down. Her cop instincts would kick in, and she'd try to help him. Barrett needed to make sure that didn't happen.

Hoping that the gunman's aim would be off from the movement of the SUV, Barrett left his door open, and while keeping it between the gunman and him, he ran to the back of the cruiser.

The shot blasted through the air.

Judging from the sound of metal slamming

into metal, the bullet had hit the door. Good. It was better than hitting him.

Still moving fast, Barrett dropped down into the ditch that he quickly discovered wasn't anywhere near dry. Because of the heavy rains the night before, there was a good five inches of mud and water. It wouldn't make running easier, but they didn't have a lot of options here. Not with the possibility of the cruiser's gas tank exploding and the gunmen closing in on them.

Another shot came, this one pinging off the back of the cruiser. It hadn't come close to hitting Della or him, and Barrett needed to make sure it stayed that way. He positioned himself on her left side, keeping his head turned so that he'd be able to see the SUV when it came closer.

And then Della and he started running.

"Keep low," he warned her though she was already doing that. Keeping watch, too, but now they were having to look behind them. He wanted to put as much distance as possible between them and the cruiser especially since the smell of gasoline was getting stronger.

More shots came, and Barrett twisted around to see the top of the SUV. He took aim as best he could and fired. It no doubt missed the gunman, but it might cause him to duck back in, which would give Della and him precious seconds to keep running. Barrett added another shot, then another.

Before a bullet came their way.

He cursed because he was too damn close, and he had no choice but to drag Della into the mud and water so they'd have some cover. Thankfully, the ditch was deep enough to keep them partially sheltered, but he heard the slow, steady crawl of the SUV coming closer. Once it reached them, the gunman would be able to pick them off like sitting ducks.

Barrett heard another sound. A welcome one this time. Backup. And Daniel was coming in hot with sirens wailing. No doubt letting Barrett, and their attackers, know that within seconds he'd be there.

More shots came, and Della and he had to duck even deeper into the ditch, until all but the top halves of their bodies were exposed. He tried not to think of how much stress this was putting on Della and the baby. He tried not to think at all except to focus on stopping the person who was sending a hail of bullets at them.

The sirens got louder, and Barrett knew that help was only seconds away. Their attackers obviously knew that as well because there was the squeal of tires on asphalt when the SUV sped away.

Barrett wanted to climb out of the ditch and

go after them, but that wasn't smart or safe. Instead, he took hold of Della's arm, lifted her and got her moving again.

He needed to warn Daniel not to get too close to the cruiser, but when Barrett reached for his phone in his pocket, he realized it was soaking wet. Likely ruined. So, he went old school, and the moment Daniel came into view, Barrett started waving his hands in a stay-back gesture.

Daniel's cruiser screeched to a stop about forty feet from them. His brother got out, taking cover behind the door. Scottie did the same on the passenger's side.

"The SUV's getting away," Daniel called out to him.

Yeah, it was, but there wasn't anything Barrett could do about that. However, he could warn Daniel and the deputy. "Get down!" Barrett shouted to them.

It wasn't a second too soon.

Because behind Della and him, the cruiser exploded.

Chapter Twelve

Della hated that she couldn't stop shaking. It was something a cop definitely shouldn't be doing. Plus, it was likely causing Barrett to worry about her even more than he should. She wasn't hurt. Nor was he. But the shock and aftereffects of the attack just wouldn't fade.

She could still hear the sound of those gunshots and the explosion. Still feel the bone-deep terror over her baby being hurt.

Barret had had those same concerns, because the moment he had her back at the sheriff's office, he'd called Dr. Tipton and asked him to come. Barrett hadn't wanted to risk taking her back to the hospital. He hadn't been able to drive her back to the ranch, either, because the CSIs and the bomb squad were on the road between town and the ranch. Della figured that being on that very road, where they'd nearly died, wouldn't help her tangled nerves.

At least she was no longer wearing her wet

muddy clothes. Esther Ridley, a deputy who worked for Barrett, had some spare clothes in her locker and lent them to Della. The jeans and cotton shirt were big on her, but at least they were dry, and Della had also managed to clean up some in the bathroom. She'd need a shower to get rid of the smell of the mud and the smoke. However, that could wait.

Barrett had changed, too, borrowing some of Daniel's things, but there were still flecks of debris from the airbag in his dark hair.

"Your blood pressure's actually good," Dr. Tipton told her. "A surprise, considering."

Yes, it was. Practically a miracle. And that seemed to steady her some.

The doctor took off the blood pressure cuff and listened to her heart. "Also good," he concluded several moments later.

Barrett was right there in his office with him, and while he wasn't exactly pacing, that's what he looked as if he wanted to do. That and explode. He definitely wasn't shaking, but the danger had lit an angry fire in him.

"Are you hurting anywhere other than the stitches on your arm?" Dr. Tipton asked.

She shook her head. Actually, that wasn't hurting nearly as much as it had, probably because the doctor had put some kind of numbing cream on it when he'd cleaned it and rebandaged it.

"Does Della need to be admitted to the hospital?" Barrett asked the doctor. There was a boatload of worry in his voice.

"No. Not unless she starts to have any cramping. Then, you'd need to bring her right in."

Cramping as in contractions, which could mean a miscarriage. That caused her stomach to tighten and her nerves to start zinging again.

"Don't worry," the doctor said. He'd obviously seen the fear in her eyes. "The baby is very protected. Everything should be fine."

Della wanted to latch on to that. But she knew nothing would be *fine* until Barrett and she stopped the men who had tried twice to kill them. Barrett obviously felt the same way because while they had been waiting on Dr. Tipton to arrive, he'd made some calls, ordering Lorraine, Rory and Curran to come in immediately for questioning. She wasn't sure they would get answers from any of them, but at least they'd know that Barrett and she weren't going to ease up on this investigation.

The doctor gathered his things and gave Della a pat on her shoulder. "Try to get some rest soon."

She would, but Della had no idea when she could work that in. She might not have a choice about it, though, since soon, very soon, she'd be dealing with an adrenaline crash. If it hit her too hard, she might have to try to take a nap on the ratty sofa in the break room.

Barrett and she thanked Dr. Tipton as he left, and the moment the doctor had shut the door behind him, Barrett eased Della into his arms. There was no heat in his hug. Just the comfort he was obviously trying to give her. Comfort that worked surprisingly well. It might have continued, too, if they hadn't heard the voice out in the squad room.

Alice.

Barrett cursed, easing away from her, and he threw open the door. Alice was making a beeline for them, and Buddy was right behind her.

"I'm sorry, boss," Buddy immediately said. "When Alice heard about the latest attack, she insisted on coming."

"Don't blame Buddy," Alice added. "I told him if I had to, I'd use one of the ranch trucks to get myself here."

Alice certainly didn't look worn down or in pain now. She looked like a terrified mother, and she went to them, hooking an arm around both Barrett and Della. The contact didn't last, though, because Barrett stepped back.

"You shouldn't have come," he snapped, and

Barrett gave Buddy a scolding glance despite Alice's insistence that he not blame the ranch hand.

Alice shook her head. "I had to. I had to see for myself that you were both all right."

"We weren't hurt," Della assured the woman, and that was as positive an explanation as she could manage.

"No." Alice muttered something. A prayer of thanks, Della realized. "But whoever's doing this just won't stop. That's why I have to do something." She paused, her breath gusting as she shifted her gaze to Barrett. "I want you to use me as bait to draw out these gunmen."

Della and Barrett groaned in unison, but Alice just talked right over their protests.

"Hear me out," she went on. "Those men obviously want me. That's why they followed me and tried to run us off the road. They could be planning to take me hostage again. Or kill me," she added in a hoarse whisper before she hiked up her chin. She was no doubt trying to look sturdier than she actually was. "Either way, you can use me to lure them out."

Della wasn't sure exactly what kind of lure Alice was suggesting, but it didn't matter. It was a bad idea. Thankfully, Barrett agreed with Della.

"No way am I putting you out there in the

line of fire," he told her. "We'll catch these guys through solid investigation and police work."

Of course, there were no guarantees of catching them, but Della had to believe that would happen. And soon.

Alice opened her mouth, no doubt to continue to plead her case for something that wasn't going to happen, but the sound of hurried footsteps stopped them. The three turned in the direction of those steps, and they spotted Lorraine, who was coming toward them. Correction, she was *storming* toward them. There was fire in her eyes, and she had that anger aimed at Alice.

"You killed Robert!" Lorraine shouted, and she launched herself at Alice, latching on to the woman's hair.

Della was so stunned that it took her a second to react. Not Barrett, though. He jumped right in, using his forearm to push Lorraine away. When that didn't work, when Lorraine continued to fight, he shoved his way in between the women, and he muscled Lorraine away.

The one-sided fight got the attention of the deputies in the squad room. Leo, Daniel and Esther hurried to assist, and it was Esther who helped stop Lorraine from charging at Alice again.

"She killed him!" Lorraine yelled, and she repeated that, her voice getting even louder, while Esther cuffed the woman.

The restraints still didn't stop Lorraine from fighting. She twisted her body, trying to wrench herself out of the cuffs while she shouted obscenities and threats at Alice. Obviously, Lorraine believed Alice had been the one to murder Casto. Or else that's what Lorraine wanted them to think, maybe so that it would take any suspicion of guilt off her.

It didn't.

Maybe Lorraine was a genuine hothead, who was likely capable of murder or hiring a hit. Of course, if this was all for show, then the woman was cold and calculating. Which also meant she could be capable of murder.

"Alice didn't kill Casto," Barrett told Lorraine, though he had to manage that over her continuing shouts. "There's proof," he added.

That caused Lorraine to finally quit fighting and go still, but there was nothing but venom in the glare that she turned on Barrett. "You're saying that because she's your mother."

He huffed. "You know my history with Alice. I'm definitely not doling out any favors to her. I don't need favors, not when I know that someone planted evidence to make her look guilty. Alice is a victim here, just like Casto."

Lorraine seemed to bite off whatever else she'd

been about to say, and her forehead bunched a moment. Maybe she was considering that. If so, then she quickly dismissed it. "You're lying," she snapped.

"No reason to lie," Barrett calmly replied. "The evidence backs me up. You, on the other hand, have no evidence to clear your name."

Lorraine practically snapped to attention. "What do you mean by that?"

"I think the comment was obvious." Again, Barrett's voice was unruffled, though Della knew there had to be plenty of emotions just beneath the surface. Lorraine could be the person who wanted them dead. "You had motive to murder your former lover because you were jealous of his relationships with other women. That also means you had motive to set up Alice. Maybe a way of killing two birds with one stone. Or rather one knife."

"I didn't kill him!" Lorraine was back to shouting.

"You have the means to hire muscle to kill," Barrett went on. "You've got the money to pay those men who've been tearing their way through this area. And let's not forget that you were once engaged to LeBeau, who was involved in this neck-deep before someone murdered him. Did you do that, Lorraine? Did you hire LeBeau to do your dirty work and then eliminate him so that he couldn't rat you out?"

If looks could have killed, Lorraine's glare and narrowed eyes would have done just that to Barrett. "I want a lawyer," she snarled through clenched teeth.

"I'll bet you do, because you need one." Barrett turned to Alice. "Do you want to file assault charges against Lorraine?"

Della certainly hadn't forgotten that Alice was standing right there, but Barrett's question caused Della to look at her. Alice was shaken up. Rightfully so. And the woman was way too pale, a reminder that, like Della, she was also recovering from her injuries.

"No," Alice said, her voice quiet. But she did aim a hard stare at Lorraine. "I didn't kill Robert, but if you lay one hand on me again, I will file charges."

That caused Lorraine to start struggling against the restraints again, and when she tried to spit at Alice, Barrett huffed. "Take Lorraine to an interview room," he told Esther. "Once she's cooled off, you can remove the restraints long enough for her to call her lawyer. After he gets here, you can question Lorraine and find out if she has an alibi for this last attack."

Of course, even if Lorraine did have an alibi, it didn't mean she was innocent since she could have hired the gunmen. Still, Della wanted the woman on the hot seat, and an interrogation would do that. With Lorraine's obvious short fuse, she might spill something incriminating.

"I also want Lorraine tested for gunshot residue," Barrett added to Esther. "If she personally took care of LeBeau, there might be some GSR still on her hands."

Good point. Something that Della wished they'd thought of earlier when Lorraine had been questioned. Still, GSR could show up even after all this time.

Esther led a cursing Lorraine away, and Barrett stayed quiet until the woman was no longer in earshot. Then, he turned to Daniel and Buddy. "I want the two of you to take Alice back to the ranch. Buddy will stay with her."

"But I want to talk about my idea for bait," Alice insisted.

Barrett gave her a look that could have frozen Hades. "No. Because there'll be no bait. If you truly want to help me and this investigation, then do it by going back to the ranch and staying put. That way, I don't have to split my attention between you and finding a killer."

Even if his words hadn't gotten through to Alice, his cop tone and look must have done the job because she gave a heavy sigh. "All right.

But keep me as sort of a backup plan. I'm willing to do whatever it takes to help."

Barrett's jaw muscles stirred in a sign of his unease. "Maybe this will help relieve any guilt you have over what happened to Casto. Someone planted your fingerprints on the knife that killed him. *Planted*," he emphasized.

Alice's breath shuddered, and she pressed her hand to her chest. "So, I'm no longer a suspect?"

Della knew that Barrett could keep the woman on his list of possible suspects, but he nodded. "You're not a suspect. Now go back to the ranch and get some rest. I'll be taking Della there soon to do the same."

Alice muttered a thank-you that obviously wasn't heartfelt. Still, Daniel didn't seem to soften. But then he probably wasn't anywhere close to the point where he could forgive and forget. Ditto for Barrett, though Della figured that being thrown together with Alice like this could break down some barriers.

That's what was happening between Barrett and her anyway.

The bad stuff that was happening was adding to the crumbling barriers. It was hard to stay distant from the father of your child when he was a decent guy and wanted to be part of your life. Well, part of the baby's life anyway.

One step at a time. Which suited Della, since she didn't know what steps to take, either.

Once Buddy, Daniel and Alice had left, Della was ready to ask Barrett for a laptop so she could help him go over the lab reports. But before that could happen, the next round of interviews came in.

Curran.

The two men in suits with him were likely lawyers.

"You want me to take this one, and you can deal with Rory when he comes in?" Leo asked, getting up from his desk and coming closer to Barrett.

"What the hell are you trying to pull now?" Curran demanded before Barrett could answer. "This is harassment, and my lawyer will be talking to the DA, the mayor and the governor."

"If you need their phone numbers, let me know," Barrett said. His voice was calm enough, but because Della was arm to arm with him, she felt his muscles tighten. "Call anyone you like, but I'm not backing down. If you've had anything to do with these attacks, I'll find out and put you in a jail cell for a very long time."

Lorraine had been all fiery hot temper, but Della could feel an even greater rage in Curran. Apparently, so could Leo, because he stepped between Curran and Barrett.

"I can do this interview," Leo offered again.

"You think because it's a different Logan doing the talking that I'll come up with something new to say?" Curran snapped. He kept his attention on Barrett. "Well, I won't, because there's nothing new. You can dig all you want, but you'll never find anything on me."

Barrett shrugged, but there was nothing casual about the gesture. The air was practically zinging between Curran and him. "Oh, I'll keep digging," Barrett assured him. "But it's time to bring in the Texas Rangers. I intend to call them today and ask for their help in the money laundering investigation."

Curran pulled back his shoulders, and now there was concern on his face. Maybe the man hadn't thought much of Barrett's cop skills, but he seemed to have some respect for, and perhaps some fear of, the Rangers.

"Are you threatening my client?" the lawyer asked.

Barrett didn't even spare him a glance. "No threat," Barrett said, his eyes still on Curran. "Just the next step in the investigation. The Rangers can put more men and resources on this than I can."

Della knew that Barrett hated to turn over control to the Rangers. That told her just how much he wanted to get Curran and have him pay for his crimes. And this was a solid next step toward doing that.

"The Rangers won't find anything, either," Curran concluded, but instead of sounding smug, there was now a worried edge in his voice. He shook his head as if to clear it. "But if you're turning it over to them, then that'll leave you some time to haul Rory in. I want to file charges against him."

Whatever she'd thought Curran might say, that wasn't it. "Charges for what?" Della asked.

"He tried to blackmail me, that's what."

"Blackmail?" Della challenged.

"Yeah," Curran confirmed. "My guess is Rory's desperate for money to pay off the loan sharks who lent him money."

Barrett huffed as if he might not be buying this. "Rory really tried to get money from you?"

"Damn right. He sugarcoated it, but he said if I'd give him a *loan*, then he'd go to Della and use his friendship with her to convince her to clear my name in these attacks and Casto's murder. I told Rory to go to hell, that I didn't need his help in clearing my name because I wasn't guilty. Not only for Casto but for anything else."

Della let all of that sink in. And it didn't sink in well. She wanted to discount anything Curran said, but if Rory was indeed that desperate, then he might have resorted to attempted blackmail.

But it wouldn't have worked. There was no way Della would allow Rory to influence the investigation, and Rory had to know that. She'd never given him even a hint that she'd been willing to bend the law.

Barrett stayed quiet several long moments before he turned to Leo. "Go ahead and take Curran into interview." He didn't add any other specific instructions, but Della knew that Leo would press for Curran's alibi for the latest attack, along with trying to push any other hot buttons he could manage.

"After we're done here, I'll have my lawyers file harassment charges," Curran threatened as Leo led him away.

Della had no doubts that Curran's attorneys would be filing those charges. But they wouldn't stick. The DA and everyone else in Mercy Ridge knew that Barrett was just doing his job. Plain and simple, Curran had the means, motive and opportunity for the attacks, and that made him a solid suspect.

"You have Rory's number?" Barrett asked her once they were alone.

She nodded and took out her phone that was now in her pocket. Unlike his cell, hers hadn't been ruined in the ditch since it had been in her bag. "You want me to call him?"

"Yeah. Find out why he's not here yet, and if

he's going to be long. I want to know if Curran is telling the truth about the blackmail attempt."

Since she wanted to know the same things, Della didn't hesitate. She considered that Rory might not answer, especially if he was already on his way here, but he answered on the first ring.

"Where are you?" Della asked, putting the call on Speaker. "You're supposed to be here for another interview."

"I know." Rory sounded strange. Scared, maybe. "I'm not sure I can make it in today."

"This interview isn't optional," Della reminded him. "Barrett and I have some questions."

"Yes, about the attack. I didn't have anything to do with that, so there's really no reason for me to come in."

"Oh, yes there is," Barrett snarled.

"Barrett," Rory muttered, and that fear level in his voice seemed to go up a significant notch. Or maybe it was just the surprise of his learning that Barrett was listening in. "I swear I don't know anything. I haven't done anything wrong."

"Curran doesn't agree," Barrett fired back. "He's here now, and he's had some…interesting things to say about you."

There was a long silence. "What did Curran say?" Rory finally asked.

"That you tried to blackmail him," Barrett supplied. "That's why you're coming in, so we can talk about that."

"I didn't blackmail him," Rory practically shouted. "I just asked him for a loan."

"Really?" Della challenged. "A loan coupled with your assurances that you'd come to me and try to sway the investigation."

"No!" This time it was a shout, and Rory repeated the denial until his breath broke in a loud groan. "I just needed the money, and Curran said if he gave it to me that he'd expect more than payment in return."

Della didn't doubt that one bit. This sounded like the truth, something that Curran had fudged to make Rory seem guilty of obstruction of justice and other charges. Of course, that didn't mean Rory was squeaky clean here. Far from it.

"You needed the money to pay off the loan sharks?" Della demanded.

"Yes." Rory answered that darn fast, but then he groaned again. "I'm in serious trouble, Della. Even worse than I was…well, before."

Della latched right on to that last word. "Before?"

Again, Rory took his time answering. "All of this started two years ago. Gambling debts," he added with plenty of disgust in his voice. "I had to borrow money then, too, but I couldn't pay it back. I was in danger of losing my business. Losing everything, including my own life. These thugs don't play nice when it comes to paying back loans."

Two years ago. That settled like a tight knot in her stomach. "You were dealing with this when Francine was still alive?"

The silence dragged on way too long, causing Barrett to snap, "Answer the question."

Rory's response was another loud groan, followed by what sounded like a broken sob. "I begged Francine to give me the money. I told her they'd kill me if I didn't pay them."

"What happened, Rory?" she asked, but Della was almost afraid to hear the answer.

"Francine wouldn't give me a dime," Rory went on a moment later. His voice and breath were broken now. "No matter how much I begged her, she wouldn't budge. She said I had to face up to what I'd done and that she wasn't going to bail me out again."

The knot twisted and tightened. So did the fist that started squeezing her heart.

"God, Rory. Did these loan sharks kill Francine?"

"No." Rory gave another hoarse sob. "No, they didn't kill her." He paused again. "I did."

Chapter Thirteen

Hell. That was Barrett's first response, followed by some much stronger profanity. All this time, for two years, Della and he had been looking for a killer, but they hadn't looked in Francine's own gene pool.

"You killed your sister?" Barrett demanded.

It took some time for Rory to say anything else, but Barrett figured that's because the man was crying. And that told him loads, that the man's confession had been the truth.

A truth that had sucker punched Della.

She had gone sheet-white and looked so wobbly that Barrett took her by the arm and had her sit down. This was no doubt bringing back the grief over losing Francine. Grief likely as fresh and raw as it had been two years ago.

"It was an accident," Rory went on, drawing Barrett's attention back to him. "Francine and I were arguing, and my gun went off. I didn't mean to shoot her. I just went over to her place to try to talk her into giving me some money, that's all. I swear I didn't mean to shoot her."

Barrett huffed when he saw a Texas-size flaw in Rory's explanation. "If you just went there to talk to her, then why'd you have a gun?"

More sobbing. "I always carry a gun, and the argument got so heated between us, I pulled it. I don't know why. Maybe I thought it'd make her realize how desperate I was."

Oh, Barrett figured that Francine had known about her brother's desperation. He also figured that Francine had told Rory a flat-out no about doling out any more cash to him. And that's when Rory had pulled a gun on her. Desperation, however, didn't excuse Rory from squat.

"You shot her when she didn't pony up money for your gambling debts?" Barrett pressed when Rory didn't say anything else for several long moments.

"No. It wasn't like that. I took out the gun, and it just went off."

Della sighed, blinked back tears. "You're a PI," she reminded the man. "You know better than to pull a gun unless you intend to use it."

"It wasn't like that!" This time he shouted it. "It wasn't like that," Rory repeated in a hoarse whisper.

Maybe, but Barrett was fed up with Rory trying to excuse himself for a horrible crime. "If it was an accident, then why didn't you report it?" Barrett snapped.

"Because I was scared, and I wasn't thinking straight. I decided to make it look like somebody had broken in."

Obviously, he'd been thinking straight enough because it *had looked* like a break-in. Rory had put his PI skills to good use to make sure the blame hadn't been put on him.

"Whether or not it was an accident, you have to come into the sheriff's office," Barrett insisted. "I'll need you to tell me what happened—on the record," he emphasized. "Bring a lawyer."

"You'll arrest me?" Rory asked.

Yeah, he would do just that. Even if Rory managed to somehow prove he hadn't intended to kill his sister, there was still the cover-up and obstruction of justice that'd followed, along with giving false statements to the cops when they'd questioned him. However, Barrett didn't want to confirm the arrest because that might cause Rory to go on the run.

"Come in right now," Barrett added, taking the phone from Della so that he could speak directly into it. He didn't want Rory to miss a word.

"I can't do that." This time Rory didn't sob, didn't shout, but there was a lot of emotion in those four words. "Someone's been following me. I suspect it's the same gunmen who tried to kill Della and you. It's not safe for me to be on the roads right now."

What a crock. If Rory had truly thought he was in danger, he would have almost certainly mentioned it earlier in the conversation before the subject of Francine had even come up.

"Come in now, or I'll issue a warrant for your arrest," Barrett told him, but he was talking to the air because Rory had already ended the call.

Cursing, Barrett handed Della back her phone and reached for his own to get that warrant. That's when he remembered his cell had been ruined in the ditch. Adding some profanity, he went to his desk and used the landline to make the call. It took him a couple of minutes to explain to the judge why he wanted it, but during his explanation, he kept his attention on Della.

She was still sitting, still looking stunned. With reason. All this time Francine's killer had been right under her nose.

Once he was finished talking to the judge, Barrett put in a quick requisition for another phone, but until it arrived, he pulled out a burner cell from his desk. Good thing he kept one there for backup, since he'd need it. He put it on the charger and went to Della.

"I'm okay," she assured him, getting to her feet.

She wasn't okay, far from it, and while Barrett didn't like to add worries of the baby to the complicated mix, he did in this case. This was yet more stress that Della just didn't need.

Barrett pulled her into his arms to try to steady her. To try to steady himself, too. And it worked. Sort of. There was certainly some soothing going on, but there was also the crackle of heat. He didn't bother cursing it because he figured it would always be there.

He still had Della against him when Daniel came in through the front door, and he made a beeline for them. A beeline complete with an expression that showed some surprise, and likely some concern, about the embrace. Thankfully, his brother didn't bring it up as Barrett eased away from Della.

"I dropped off Alice and Buddy," Daniel told him. "No signs of a break-in or anything, but I saw Josh, and he said he saw someone down by the back fence of your pasture. He said the guy took off when he spotted him."

Barrett went on instant alert. Josh Jenkins was a part-time ranch hand, one with a good eye. "Did he get a description?"

"Only that it was a man wearing dark clothes."

That put plenty of alarm back in Della's face. "Should we go back there to be with Alice?"

"I told Josh to stay close," Daniel explained

before Barrett could answer, "and I'm sending over one of my hands to keep watch."

Those were good security measures, but Barrett figured neither Alice nor Buddy would be relaxing any until he was there. Unfortunately, that meant taking Della back out since he had no intentions of leaving her here.

"When Esther and Leo finish with the interviews, Della and I will head out," Barrett said. Maybe Lorraine and Curran would have given them something they could use to blow this case wide-open.

Maybe with the finger pointing at Rory.

If he could keep killing his sister a secret all this time, there was no telling what else he was capable of hiding. After all, his desperation over his loans was still there. But what motive would Rory have had for orchestrating the attacks and killing Casto? None.

Well, unless Curran had put him up to doing it.

If so, then Curran had thrown Rory under the bus by telling Della and him that Rory had tried to blackmail him.

Barrett's desk phone rang, and he thought maybe it was the judge's office calling with the arrest warrant. It wasn't. When he answered, the person on the other end of the line stayed silent for several moments.

"We need to talk," the person finally said. It

was a man, and his voice was low with a growl to it.

"Who is this?" Barrett asked.

Another long pause. "I'm the man who's been trying to kill you. And like I said, we need to talk."

DELLA HADN'T HEARD what the caller said to Barrett, but she immediately noticed the change in him. He sandwiched the phone between his ear and shoulder while he riffled through his desk and came up with a recorder. The moment he flicked it on, he also put the call on speaker.

"You're the man who's been trying to kill Deputy Howell and me?" he asked.

That question sent both Daniel and her closer to the phone, and Della held her breath, waiting. Thankfully, she didn't have to wait long.

"I'm the man *someone hired* to kill you both. Casto, too," the man corrected. "I got nothing personal against the deputy and you."

Well, it sure as heck felt personal to her. Especially with her baby put in danger. That sent a surge of anger through her. She was pretty sure Barrett was feeling that, too, because the muscles in his face had turned to iron.

"Who are you?" Barrett demanded.

"I'd rather not give you my name, not over the phone, but like I said, we need to talk. All of this is getting out of hand, and you came damn close to killing me earlier. This was supposed to be a one and done. You weren't supposed to survive the first attack."

Della hadn't thought the rage inside her could bubble up even more, but it did.

"Who hired you?" Barrett pressed.

"I'll give you that. Well, I'll give you what I can anyway, but like I said, not over the phone. We have to meet."

Barrett made a sound of disgust. "Why, so you can try to kill me again?"

"Nope. I'm offering you the real deal. A chance to put an end to all of this mess. In exchange I want a deal that I figure you can work out with the DA. I don't expect to skate. I figure I'll do some jail time, but it won't be life or a needle in the arm. Jail time for me, and in exchange you'll get the person who's behind this."

Oh, mercy. What a decision. No way did Della want this snake getting anything less than the death penalty, but she also didn't want the attacks to go on. She wanted—no, she needed— to get on with her life. That was the best chance she had of keeping the baby safe.

"All right," Barrett finally said to the caller. "Let's talk. But FYI, I won't be meeting you out in the sticks or someplace where you can gun me down."

"Okay," he answered. "But I want you to bring Deputy Howell with you."

"No deal." Barrett didn't hesitate. "It's me and you, or this meeting doesn't happen."

Apparently, the man had to think about that because he didn't say anything for a long time. "Just you and me," he agreed. "And it won't be in the sticks. I'll meet you at the Drop In Diner just up the street in ten minutes."

"You're at the diner." Barrett sounded skeptical, but he motioned for Daniel to get moving. No doubt so he could see if the man was actually there.

"I'm nearby, and I'll see you coming. Like I said, make sure you're alone. This isn't a setup. I need to make a deal with you. Come now," the man added, and he ended the call.

Barrett made a quick call to have someone trace the number, though they both knew the guy was almost certainly using a disposable cell that couldn't be traced. Still, it was something they had to rule out.

"This is the number of my phone," Barrett said, scribbling it down on a piece of paper that he handed to her. "Stay put, and I mean it. I'll have backup, but I don't want it to be you."

Della wanted to help him, but she couldn't. Too risky. That also meant it was too risky for Barrett, too.

"You have to be safe. You have to take precautions," she insisted.

"I will," he assured, and as if it were the most natural thing in the world, he brushed a kiss on her mouth. "Text Daniel and tell him to stay out of sight and on this side of the street."

The diner was on the opposite side of Main Street, but that didn't mean that's where the gunman was waiting and watching. In fact, he could be anywhere. He might not even be near Mercy Ridge. Or he could be on the roof of a building that would give him a good shot at taking out Barrett.

"If Esther and Leo finish the interviews, have everyone stay put inside the building," he added.

She wanted to repeat her warning for him to be careful, but she knew he would be. Plus, he was already heading out. Not through the front of the building but out back as Daniel had done.

Della immediately felt the fear wash over her in heavy, fast waves. Oh, God. Barrett had to be all right. He just had to be.

It was too risky for her to go right to the windows, but while keeping her hand over her weapon, Della went to the corner of the squad room. She stayed back, out of the direct line of sight of anyone outside. However, she could see out.

There was a handful of people milling around,

but almost immediately she saw them duck into the various businesses that lined Main Street. Daniel or Barrett had likely put out the warning for everyone to get inside. What Della couldn't see was either Daniel or Barrett. She figured that was a good thing, and maybe it meant they were keeping out of the path of a would-be attack.

"What the hell's going on?" she heard Curran bellow from the hall.

Della ignored him, though she did hear Leo explain that there could be a gunman outside. If Curran had been the one to hire the thug, then hearing that might cause him great concern. After all, if this was legit, if the hired gun really did want to deal, then he could possibly ID Curran as his boss.

A few moments later, Leo came to her. He, too, had drawn his weapon and was alone. Apparently, Curran had decided to heed the warning and stay put. But she did hear the man having a muffled conversation either with his lawyers or someone he'd called. Della half listened, hoping to catch something incriminating, but she kept her gaze pinned to Main Street.

The seconds crawled by.

And with each one, Della had to remind herself to tamp down her breathing and steady her heartbeat. Not just because it wouldn't do any good but also because of the added stress it might cause for the baby. Her stress went up a significant notch, though, when she heard the next sound.

A shout.

"Don't!" a man yelled.

And it was quickly followed by something else Della definitely didn't want to hear. A gunshot. Then, another. Not on Main Street. The shots seemed to have come from the back of the sheriff's office.

Now the terror came in a hot sticky wave over her, and her first thought was Barrett. God, had he been shot? She wanted to rush out, to hurry and try to help him, but she could be walking straight into an ambush.

Leo didn't stay put, though. "Keep watch of the front door," he barked out, and he hurried toward the back.

It took every ounce of willpower to stay put. This wasn't busywork, she told herself. She needed to make sure whoever had fired that shot didn't come rushing in and try to take them out. Still, she hated not knowing what was happening.

Della finally released the breath she'd been holding when she caught sight of Barrett and Daniel. Barrett was running toward the back of the building. Right toward the sound of those shots. Daniel rushed in through the front door.

"Barrett's okay," he muttered as he ran past her, heading in the same direction that Leo had taken.

"Stay put," she heard Esther say several moments later.

The deputy was no doubt talking to Lorraine. Maybe the woman would listen because right now, they didn't need anyone else distracting them. Especially a distraction from someone who was a suspect in the attacks.

"Leo texted me to lock the front door," Esther said.

That didn't help steady Della's nerves because it meant Barrett thought there was still danger. And there likely was. It'd been a couple of minutes since Della had heard those shots, but the gunman could still be nearby.

With the front of the building secured, Della followed Esther to the back, past Curran, who scowled at her. Past the interview room where Lorraine was waiting in the doorway. Esther went to the back door just as Daniel opened it.

And Della saw Barrett.

Alive and unharmed, thank God.

But someone else wasn't. She saw the blood. Then, the man sprawled out on the ground. If he wasn't already dead, he soon would be, thanks to the slugs he'd taken in the chest.

Barrett glanced at her, motioning for her to stay back. Della did, but by looking over Esther's shoulder, she could take it all in. Leo, Barrett and Daniel were there—their weapons trained not on the guy on the ground but on another man. He had a bulky build and was wearing dark jeans and a black T-shirt. He was also on his knees, his hands tucked behind his head. Or at least they were until Barrett moved in to cuff the guy.

In the distance, Della heard the wail of an ambulance. Since it was coming from just up the street, it wouldn't take long to get here.

"What happened?" Esther asked.

"These are the two men who tried to kill Della and me," Barrett answered.

"I didn't know my partner was going to show up here," the cuffed man volunteered. He gave a dry sneer. "Guess he didn't like the notion of me trying to cut a deal with the sheriff."

"You shot him?" Esther added to Barrett.

"No." Barrett tipped his head to the other man. "He did."

"Yeah, I did, when he tried to kill me first to shut me up," the guy verified. "And now I'm ready to talk."

Chapter Fourteen

Barrett had Leo and Esther wait with the dead guy while he ushered the gunman inside. He made a quick check on Della. Thank God she wasn't hurt, but she sure as heck could have been when those thugs started shooting. Those bullets had gone way too close to the building.

"Get a crime scene unit out here," Barrett instructed Leo and Esther, though he was certain his brother was already doing that. Leo was on the phone with someone while he continued to keep watch around them. It seemed the danger had passed.

Seemed.

But Barrett didn't want anyone taking any unnecessary chances, especially Della. And that's why he motioned for her to go ahead of them. She did, but the gunman and she still managed to exchange long glances as they made their way up the hall and to an interview room.

There was plenty of anger in Della's eyes, and

Barrett was sure it was mirrored in his own. If this fool was truly a hired gun as he claimed, he'd come damn close to killing Della and him not once but twice. Della was still sporting the proof of that—the injury on her arm from their encounter.

They passed Lorraine and Curran on the short walk. Both were standing in the doorways of the two interview rooms. One of which Barrett now needed.

"You two can go," Barrett told Curran and Lorraine. Curran opened his mouth to say something, but Barrett shut him down with a glance. "Leave now," Barrett insisted.

The moment that Curran and his lawyers walked out, Barrett ushered the gunman into one of the rooms. He didn't handle the guy with kid gloves but instead let him drop down into the chair. He'd already taken his gun and had searched him, but Barrett now looked at the ID that was in his wallet.

"Cedric Ezell," Barrett read aloud, and that sent Daniel to the laptop in the corner, no doubt to do a run on the man's background. Barrett was betting he wasn't squeaky clean.

To keep everything legal, Barrett read the man his rights and turned on the recorder. He waited for Ezell to start squawking for a lawyer, but he didn't. That might change though if this *chat* didn't go the way he wanted.

"I'm listening," Barrett said, taking the seat across from Ezell. Della stayed standing, her hard stare drilling into Ezell.

"You gotta take murder off the table," Ezell started. "And that should be easy to do since I didn't kill anybody."

"Really?" Barrett didn't bother to sound as if he believed that.

"Really," Ezell verified. "Donnell did the killings. Donnell Lawler," he provided. "He's the dead guy out back."

Barrett glanced over his shoulder to confirm that Daniel was running Lawler, too. "So, your partner did the murders, and you stood by and watched?"

Ezell lifted his shoulder. "It's the way things worked out. I was the driver, mostly."

It was the *mostly* that caused Barrett's blood to boil. So did what he saw on the laptop screen when Daniel brought it over. Yeah, both Ezell and Lawler had sheets a mile long. Nothing as serious as murder, but there were plenty of arrests for assaults, including one with a deadly weapon. Both had worked as bouncers and that catchall of "personal security."

"Take murder off the table," Ezell repeated, "and I'll tell you everything you want to know."

It was tempting. Mercy, was it. Barrett wanted answers, bad, but he didn't want this idiot to walk. "Convince me that you didn't kill anyone," Barrett said. That was a start. Maybe if he got the guy talking, he'd spill his guts. "Then, and only then, will I consider a deal."

Barrett could practically see the wheels turning in Ezell's head. How much to say. How much to leave out. This thug would do or say whatever it took to try to save his own hide.

"Somebody hired LeBeau, Donnell and me to do a job," Ezell finally started. "We were supposed to rough up Casto. *Rough him up*," he emphasized. "Not kill him. We had orders to rough up his woman, too. Alice Logan. And then we were told to dump them in the woods outside of town."

Barrett didn't say anything. He just gave Ezell a flat look and made a circling motion with his index finger to indicate he wanted him to keep going.

Ezell dragged in a long breath. "LeBeau went crazy or something. I think he was high. Or maybe needing a fix 'cause he uses sometimes. Anyway, we had Casto all trussed up, but he spit in LeBeau's face. LeBeau grabbed a knife and stabbed him. I swear, he stabbed him right there on the ground. I couldn't believe it. I asked LeBeau if he'd lost his mind, and he came after me. He might have killed me, too, if Donnell hadn't pulled him off me."

Barrett could maybe see things playing out like this. *Maybe.* "Why were you supposed to rough up Casto and Alice?"

"Don't know," Ezell readily answered. "I don't know," he repeated when Barrett glared at him and huffed. "I didn't ask why. I just needed the money. I got a boatload of back child support due, and my ex is hounding me."

Barrett hated to think of this scum having children, but it was a reminder that anyone could father a child. He had, and he didn't have any qualifications to make him a good dad. Something he pushed aside, since he didn't need that distraction in his head right now.

From the corner of his eye, he saw Della shift her position, and she leaned closer to Ezell, putting her fisted hands on the table. "Maybe your dead friend, Donnell, had a theory about why you were hired to do it."

Ezell lifted his shoulder again. "If he did, he didn't say."

Barrett doubted that. The pair had had plenty of time together, and even if they hadn't discussed it before Casto's murder, they sure as heck would have afterward. Too bad Barrett couldn't have been a fly on the wall because he needed to know. Of course, once he had the name of the person who'd paid these goons, then he'd have all the answers he needed.

If Curran was behind this, he could have maybe hoped to use Casto's and Alice's attack to distract Barrett, to get him off the trail of the money laundering investigation. It was just as possible, though, that Casto knew plenty about that illegal operation. And maybe Curran had wanted to teach the man a lesson of some sort.

But there were also Lorraine and Rory to consider.

No fury like a woman scorned in Lorraine's case. And Rory, well, he'd had a secret that he wanted to keep hidden. He'd killed his own sister. So, Ezell and crew could be connected to that.

"What happened after LeBeau killed Casto?" Barrett asked to get the interview moving along again.

"Well, we kind of panicked at first. Then, LeBeau said we oughta set up the woman, Alice. He said everybody would think she'd done it anyway 'cause Casto and she got in a fight or something."

Yes, some might indeed believe Alice had done it. Barrett had strongly considered that possibility. In fact, before he'd cleared her, thanks to the proof of planted fingerprints, she'd been at the top of his suspect list.

"We were all wearing gloves," Ezell went on, "but LeBeau dragged Alice over to Casto's body. She was out like a light then 'cause LeBeau had hit her on the head. And he pressed her fingers on the handle so she'd get the blame."

That meshed with the evidence. Barrett wouldn't mention, though, that the setup had failed when the lab had discovered the planted prints.

"And then what happened?" Barrett pressed.

This time, Ezell didn't pause to think. "We left. Me and Donnell started walking toward his SUV and LeBeau headed toward his. LeBeau wasn't parked near us so we went in opposite directions." But now he hesitated. "Once we were out of earshot of LeBeau, Donnell called the boss and went over what happened. When Donnell hung up, he said he had orders to take care of something with LeBeau. He left, and a while later he came back and told me that Le-Beau was dead."

That, too, meshed with the evidence. Of course, it could have been Ezell who'd killed LeBeau, but with Donnell dead, there might not be any proof of it.

"Why'd your boss want LeBeau dead?" Della asked.

Ezell's response was another shoulder shrug. "Donnell didn't say."

No, but Barrett could guess about this part. The boss had been pissed off that his or her orders hadn't been carried out. Instead of a "roughing up," this had turned into a murder, and if Barrett was to believe Ezell's story, then LeBeau was to blame for turning an assault and kidnapping into murder.

"Why go after Sheriff Logan and me?" Della asked. Her voice stayed flat, a cop's voice, but Barrett knew there was plenty of emotion beneath the surface. "Why try to kill us?"

"Donnell said it was orders. I was to drive. He fired the shots. The boss didn't want you and the sheriff digging into stuff. Donnell said he was told it was best if you two were out of commission."

Out of commission. A polite word for dead. And not just their deaths, either, but also their child's.

Barrett had to take a minute to rein in his fury. Fury that he wanted to unleash on this idiot seated across from him. But while that might give him some temporary relief, it wouldn't fix things.

"If what you've told me is true, I might be able to talk the DA into taking murder charges off the table," Barrett finally said. "You'll still do jail time." In fact, he could do a lot of jail time because accessory to murder could carry the same penalty as the crime itself.

Now Barrett was the one who leaned in, and he got right in Ezell's face. "If I find out that anything you've told me is a lie, then there'll be no deal. You'll go down for two counts of murder and multiple counts of attempted murder on two police officers and a civilian."

"I've told you the truth," Ezell insisted. "So, it's a deal?"

"I'll go to bat for you," Barrett assured, and he wondered if Ezell had a clue that a cop could lie during an interview. Barrett wasn't lying, not exactly. He wanted this thug's boss more than the thug. But it'd settle better with him and likely Della, too, if everyone involved in this faced maximum charges.

Ezell stared at him as if trying to suss out if Barrett was trying to pull something over on him. Then, he finally nodded.

"Give me the name of the person who hired you," Barrett demanded. "That'll go a long way toward getting me to really go to bat for you."

Ezell nodded again and dragged in a long breath that it seemed he was going to need. "My boss is Rory Silva."

Even though Barrett had steeled himself up, it still felt like a punch to the gut. Della had been best friends with Rory's sister. She'd grieved with him. Or at least she thought that's what was happening. But it was all a sham, since Rory had been the one to kill Francine. Now, if he was to believe Ezell, Rory was trying to kill them, too.

"There's an arrest warrant in the works for Rory," Barrett told Daniel when his brother got up and took out his phone. "But I'll try to contact him again and try to *coax* him into giving himself up."

"And what about this guy?" Daniel asked. "You want me to book him?"

Barrett went over his options. "Go ahead and put him in lockup." They could hold Ezell for forty-eight hours before charging him with anything. Of course, during that time the man would likely wise up and ask for a lawyer. Still, Barrett had gotten what he wanted from him. "After I've talked with Rory and the DA, we'll settle on the charges."

And those charges for Ezell would be legion. Maybe not murder if Barrett did try going for the deal, but there'd be plenty of other felonies.

While Daniel hauled Ezell away, Barrett took Della to his office. He needed to use his desk phone to try to find Rory, but first he wanted to make sure Della was as steady as she could be. She was putting up a good front, but that didn't stop him from shutting the door and pulling her into his arms. He brushed a chaste kiss on the top of her head, too. It didn't feel exactly chaste to him, but then this was Della.

"Rory," she whispered on a hoarse breath.

Yeah, there was the emotion that he knew would come. Rory had betrayed her. Worse, he was a killer. At least according to Ezell he was. Barrett really needed to talk to Rory to see if what the man said meshed with the statement Ezell had given them.

"But at least now we know who killed Francine," she went on.

Della practically melted into his arms, and Barrett was glad she seemed to find some kind of comfort there. Forty-eight hours ago, she definitely wouldn't have let him do something like this.

She'd have to let him do more, of course. More for her, more for the baby. But that was a topic for another time.

"And with one gunman dead and the other behind bars, this could be the end of the attacks," he reminded her. Barrett wouldn't mention that Rory or whoever had orchestrated this could possibly hire more thugs to try to finish the job.

Della eased back a bit and stared up at him with her intense blue eyes. "You believe Ezell?"

"I want to believe him," Barrett settled for saying, and he would have added more, a reassurance that even if it wasn't the truth, they'd get to the bottom of this soon enough, but the knock at the door stopped him.

Cursing softly, Barrett let go of Della so he could answer it. He expected to see one of his deputies, but it wasn't.

It was Lorraine. And she was alone. Her lawyer wasn't anywhere in sight.

"You're free to go for now," Barrett reminded her.

Lorraine nodded, but then she stepped inside, shutting the door behind her. "I need you to see something. I didn't want to give it to your deputy, so I waited until I could speak to you."

Barrett automatically moved in front of Della when Lorraine reached into her purse. Lorraine noticed his shift, too, and her eyes widened.

"I don't have a gun," she insisted. "And I'm not here to hurt either of you. In fact, I think this will help with your investigation." Lorraine pulled out a USB storage device and handed it to him. "There are documents and files on there that prove Wilbur Curran participated in a money laundering scheme."

Barrett eyed both Lorraine and the USB device with plenty of skepticism. "Really?"

"Really," she verified. "Robert was involved, too, but now that he's dead, that doesn't matter." Her eyes welled up with tears, and she swallowed hard. If Lorraine was faking her grief over Casto, then she was good at it. "There's no reason for me to protect Robert any longer."

Barrett stared at her for a long moment. "Casto and Curran were partners in the money laundering?"

"No, not partners. But Robert let Curran use his real estate business to wash some of the funds. And no, I don't know where Curran got the money. That's not in the files. He just funneled some cash, and Robert kept track of it."

Barrett glanced at Della to see her take on this, but she was obviously as surprised as he was. "Why are you doing this?" Della asked.

Lorraine touched her fingers to her trembling mouth. "Because you believe Curran killed Robert, and if he did do that, use what I've given you to arrest him. Then, find a way to make him pay for killing the man I loved."

Chapter Fifteen

The thoughts were whirling around in Della's mind. So much had happened in the last few hours that it was hard for her to focus. But it was definitely something she had to do, because she had to keep watch as Barrett and she drove back to the ranch.

The hired guns were out of the picture, but that didn't mean there couldn't be others. After all, Rory was still at large, and if he'd truly hired Ezell and his partner, he could hire others. Ditto for Curran. And then there was their third suspect—Lorraine—and what she'd given them.

"Do you believe Lorraine was telling the truth about why she gave us that dirt on Curran?" Della asked Barrett.

Now that they'd had a couple of hours to process what was on the USB and the details Ezell had given them in the interview, Della was hoping his mind was clearer than hers. Like her, though, he was keeping watch as well, and she was certain Daniel was doing the same as he followed behind them in another cruiser.

"The info on the USB looks legit," he answered after a long pause. Though it would be up to the computer geeks at the Ranger lab to determine that. "Maybe she wants to get back at Curran. Maybe she just wants suspicion on someone other than herself."

Yes, that was Della's take, too, and it caused her to let out a weary sigh. It was hard to know the woman's actual motives, but Lorraine had seemed genuinely broken up about Casto's death. Still, that didn't mean she hadn't hired Ezell and the others for a "roughing up" job that got out of hand.

Della breathed a little easier when Barrett took the final turn to his ranch. Ironic, that just hours ago seeing his place had been a source of added stress. But no more. The barrier was no longer there between Barrett and her. Along with the heat from the attraction, there was also, well, a bond between them. A baby could do that.

Could cause other problems, too.

Along with everything else on his plate, Barrett was no doubt dealing with the pregnancy, and that meant soon they were going to have to talk about it.

When Barrett's house came into view, Della

got a jolt of fresh adrenaline the moment she spotted the Culver Crossing cruiser. "Jace is here," she said, recognizing the vehicle. "Something must be wrong."

Barrett must have thought so, too, because he motioned for Daniel to wait in his own cruiser while Della and he hurried into the house. They found Jace all right, along with Buddy and Alice. They all appeared to be fine.

"I was just about to call you," Jace told her. "I'm taking Alice back to my place, and I'll bring in a reserve deputy to guard her."

"I thought it was best if I got out from under your feet," Alice quickly added, her comment aimed at Barrett.

Barrett stayed quiet a moment, probably figuring out the best way to respond. He likely didn't want to say something along the lines of "you're welcome to stay as long as needed." No. Because he was as uncomfortable with her being here as Alice was.

"You've got the manpower to guard her?" Barrett asked Jace.

"I'll make do," Jace assured him. He tipped his head to Della. "You okay?"

She nodded. "But we have a lot of updates on the investigation. Barrett and I just did the report before we left his office, and we copied you on it."

"I was reading it while Alice was getting ready to go. Once Rory's found, maybe things can start getting back to normal."

Yes, and that included her going back to work. Della wasn't sure she was ready for that just yet.

"I can have Daniel follow you to Culver Crossing," Barrett offered.

"Appreciate it," Jace said, and he headed for the door. Buddy did, too, telling Barrett to call him if he needed him.

Alice paused a moment, her gaze lingering on Barrett. "Thank you for everything."

He huffed as if insulted that she'd thank him for doing his job, but then his expression softened just a little. "Stay safe," he muttered. It wasn't exactly warm and fuzzy, but it did seem to be a step toward thawing their relationship.

"Wait here," Barrett told Della, and he went to the cruiser to have a word with Daniel. No doubt to explain that he wanted Daniel to provide some backup on the drive to Culver Crossing. Della was thankful for the extra security measure, but maybe it wouldn't be needed. Maybe the danger was truly over.

Maybe.

When he was finished talking to his brother, Barrett came back to the house, locked the door and reset the security system. He definitely seemed in "let's get to work" mode because he headed straight for the laptop on the kitchen table.

"You should eat and get some rest," he told her, his attention on what he was reading on the screen.

Della got a bottle of water from the fridge, but she didn't want either rest or food right now. She'd eaten just a few hours earlier in Barrett's office when Leo had ordered sandwiches from the diner. And as for rest, that wouldn't happen with her thoughts going a mile a minute. Still, she did want to see if there were any updates on the case, so she went to Barrett and read from over his shoulder. Della instantly saw the reason he muttered some profanity.

Rory was still nowhere to be found.

And Curran had called the sheriff's office to blast Barrett about the so-called evidence Lorraine had given them. Curran hadn't had the number to Barrett's burner cell or he would have no doubt contacted him directly.

"How'd Curran find all of this out so soon?" Della asked. She had a long drink of the water, then set the bottle aside.

"Probably from Lorraine herself. She might have wanted to gloat that she'd given us something to put him away. Curran's lawyer will fight any arrest warrant," he added after a moment.

Of course, he would. No way would he just

allow himself to be locked up. And the trouble was, the evidence was questionable. There was no chain of custody on it, which meant there was no way to verify if someone had tampered with the info so it might not hold up in court. Still, unless the info on there was completely false, there was finally some proof that Curran was dirty. That was a start anyway.

"This could make Curran…desperate," Barrett went on. "If he's the one who actually hired Ezell and the others, then this could spur him to make another attempt. Not just to take out Ezell, but us, too."

Yes, Curran could hire more gunmen for that. Then again, maybe Curran and his lawyers would stay busy enough with the legal wrangling so Curran wouldn't have time to put together something like that.

"Eliminating us won't help Curran," Della said. "The Rangers will still go after him."

Barrett nodded but then looked back at her when she made a slight sound of pain as she reached for the water bottle. "You're hurting," he said, getting to his feet. There was plenty of alarm suddenly on his face.

"No. It was just a twinge, that's all."

He gave her a flat look, clearly not buying that, and he glanced down at the bandage. He couldn't see the actual stitches, but the area around the bandage was no longer an angry red color.

Barrett cursed again, probably remembering the attack that'd led to her injury. She hated that he was likely beating himself up about that, and Della reached up to try to smooth away the worry line on his bunched up forehead.

"You really don't have to worry about me," she said.

His expression said otherwise. Barrett's eyes were stormy gray now and nailed to her. And just like that, the moment changed. His worry morphed into something else. Just as intense. But definitely different, and she recognized it, too.

The lust.

He stepped back as if fighting it, but Della didn't want him to gather enough willpower to move away from her. They'd been dealing with this attraction, well, for as long as they'd known each other, and she knew she would feel a heck of lot better in his arms than out of them.

She moved in, came up on her tiptoes and kissed him.

It took a couple of heartbeats, but she felt him lose the battle, and his mouth crush hers. The kiss was hard, almost brutal and in direct contrast to his touch. He slid his arm around her waist and eased her to him with surprising gentleness. A gentleness she wasn't sure she wanted. Barrett was treating her like glass, and she wanted him to treat her like his lover.

Della helped remedy that. She deepened the kiss and pressed her body against his, making sure there was pressure in all the right places. And Barrett reacted all right. There was a low rumble in his throat, and she felt the leash snap on his self-control.

Good.

That was her first thought, but soon she had trouble thinking at all. Her body just reacted. She forgot all about the nightmare they'd been through. Forgot about her injury and that she was pregnant. Instead, she let herself slide right into the heat he was offering.

And he was offering plenty.

The kiss became hungry, and soon it wasn't enough. She wanted more. To touch him. To have him take her as he'd done so many times before. Della started to tell him that but then realized it wasn't necessary.

Without breaking the kiss, Barrett scooped her up in his arms and headed for the bedroom.

BARRETT FIGURED HE should take a moment and reconsider what he was doing. But he didn't want to reconsider. He wanted Della, and a moment or two of thinking about that wasn't going to change things.

Apparently, not for Della, either.

She certainly didn't hesitate when she hooked her good arm around his neck and used the leverage to pull his mouth closer to hers. Not that it could get closer, but she certainly tried.

The ache was already there. The need. And despite everything that had gone on, the fire was even hotter than usual. Maybe because he'd gone so long without her. His body was already urging him on, but he forced himself to be gentle when he eased her down onto the bed.

Della didn't bother with gentle when she caught onto his shirt to get it off him. Figuring it would be better for her arm, Barrett just shoved up her top, pushed down the cups of her bra and kissed her breasts. Those kind of kisses had always revved her up fast, and now was no different.

She arched her body, pushing her hips against his. That revved him, too, and let him know that this was going to be fast. Too fast. But that was the trouble when the need was this strong.

Moving her hand between them, she unzipped him and slid her palm down into his boxers. Barrett hadn't needed anything else to kick up the fire a notch, but that did it. It also let him know that he had to do something about getting them at least partially naked.

He got off her, not easily, because Della was still touching him, but he finally maneuvered enough to shimmy off her loose jeans and shoes. Her panties came next, but he took a moment to drop some kisses on her stomach. And he tried not to think of the pregnancy.

Barrett failed.

He definitely thought about it. Della must have felt his hesitation because she shook her head and went after his jeans.

"We're doing this," she insisted. "Pregnant women might not get to have multiple cups of coffee, but we can have sex."

For some reason that made him smile. Not for long, though. That's because she managed to shove down his jeans and boxers, and then dragged him back down on top of her. It didn't take much encouragement for that to happen. Barrett was already primed and ready to go.

Despite her hands and mouth urging him on, Barrett went slow. And stayed gentle when he slipped inside her. The sensations nearly robbed him of his breath. Yes, it'd been too long without her.

Della kept up the urging, lifting herself to meet his strokes when he began to move inside her. He knew her body so well. Knew that she was already close to the peak. Part of him wanted to draw out the pleasure, to linger until maybe some of this heat inside him had cooled.

But he couldn't.

Della made a sound of silky pleasure, and she released the grip she had on him to fist her hands in her hair. Her eyelids fluttered down. Her mouth opened. Her face flushed. And she went straight over the edge.

With her body closing around him like a fist, Barrett had no choice but to go with her.

He didn't rush his coming back from the ripples of pleasure. Barrett kept the intimate contact, though he did put some of his weight on his forearms so that he wouldn't crush her.

"I needed that," she whispered. "Thanks."

She made another sound, a low moan this time, and he knew the drill. Della wasn't much of a postsex cuddler and would soon drift off to sleep. Good. Because she needed the rest. Barrett did, too, but he'd skip it and get some work done once he was sure she was sacked out.

He shifted his position again, dropping down beside her on the bed. She didn't stir, but since she was nearly naked, he lifted the side of the quilt and laid it over her. However, when he went to get off the bed, her good arm came around him, pulling him closer. Apparently, she was in a cuddling mood after all.

Barrett snuggled her against him, her head fitting right into the curve of his neck. It was perfect. A reminder of everything he'd missed when they'd been apart these past two months. But he couldn't help thinking—was this temporary?

Della and he hadn't really resolved anything between them. Yes, the sex had been damn good, but they hadn't talked about the future. About the baby. In a little more than six months, they'd be parents, and while that gave them plenty of time to work out how they were going to handle parenthood, he thought he would need every minute of those months to come to terms with it.

He hoped like the devil that he didn't screw this up.

Della's breathing soon settled into a slow, familiar rhythm. Her muscles relaxed. That should have been his cue to get up and get to work, but he didn't budge. In fact, he closed his own eyes, figuring that a little nap wouldn't hurt.

Barrett wasn't sure how long he'd been asleep, but he woke with a jolt when he heard the sound of ringing. It took him a moment to fight through his hazy mind and determine it was Della's phone—which was somewhere on the floor in the heap of their clothes.

Della stirred, too, muttering something incoherent, but she crawled over him to get to the side of the bed. She reached down, took her phone from her jeans pocket and blinked while she looked at the screen.

"It's Jace," she said.

Since this could be business, Barrett didn't curse, but he did glance at the clock on the bedside table. Then, he did curse. Because his nap had lasted over two hours. Outside, it was already dark.

"Yeah?" Della answered, sounding as groggy as she looked. However, she did remember to put the call on speaker.

"Is Barrett there with you?" Jace immediately asked. "Are you both all right?"

"Yes on both counts." There was a quick shift in Della's posture. She sat up, and she suddenly looked very much like the cop that she was. "Why?"

"Good." Jace muttered some profanity, too. "Because we've had some trouble."

Chapter Sixteen

Trouble.

That was the one word that came through loud and clear, and Della could tell from Jace's tone that whatever had happened was bad. Her relaxed muscles tensed again, and she went on instant alert.

"What happened?" she asked.

"It's Alice." Jace muttered some more profanity. "I dropped her and the reserve deputy off at her house a couple of hours ago and told her to stay put. Apparently, she didn't."

Sweet heaven. That definitely wasn't good. The person who'd hired those gunmen was still out there. Was still a threat.

"Where'd she go?" Barrett snapped. He got up from the bed and started to get dressed. Della did the same.

"I'm not sure. The reserve deputy, Crystal Rankin, said that Alice went to her bedroom to lie down. Crystal thought all was well, but when she went to check on Alice about two hours later, she found a note that Alice had left on her bed. Apparently, someone called Alice and convinced her that both Barrett and you had been taken hostage."

"What?" Barrett snapped, anger and shock in his tone.

"Yeah," Jace verified. "She wrote in the note that she took some money from her safe to pay a ransom and that she was going to save both of you."

Della wasn't sure whose groan was louder—hers or Barrett's. "Who convinced her to go out?" Barrett pressed.

"Don't know. But Alice said something else in the note. She said she had to save the baby, her grandchild." Jace paused. "Della, are you pregnant?"

How the heck had Alice learned about the baby? Della definitely hadn't wanted to tell him this way, and she couldn't take the time to think of a better response, so she just said, "Yes." Later, though, she'd want to talk to him about it. Would want to ask Alice, too, how she'd known. But for now, they had a more serious problem.

"How long has Alice been gone?" Della asked, not only to get Jace to shift subjects but also because she truly wanted to know.

"About two hours at most, judging from the

time she was out of Crystal's sight. I've been trying to call her, but she or someone else turned off her phone."

Della was betting it was the *someone else*. If Alice had believed they were in danger, she would have kept her phone on in case Barrett or she tried to contact the woman.

"I'm at Alice's place now," Jace went on, "but there's no sign of her. She didn't use her car, but it's possible she met this person at the end of the road. That way, Crystal wouldn't have heard anyone pull up. The bedroom window is unlocked so that's probably how she got out."

Yes, that was possible, but this still didn't make sense. "How could someone have convinced Alice that we'd been taken hostage? Better yet, why wouldn't she have called Barrett or me to verify that?"

"Again, I don't know. Maybe she wasn't thinking straight. Maybe this person convinced her that if she called you, it could get you killed."

Della thought about Alice's head injury that'd been serious enough for her to stay in the hospital. That might be playing into all of this. That and the recent psychological trauma she'd experienced. Still, it didn't make sense that she'd fall for something like this.

"I've called in every deputy available," Jace

went on. "Barrett, I'm asking you to do the same."

"Of course," Barrett assured him. "But if this is an attempt to get to Della and me, then I figure very soon we'll be getting a call from the kidnapper."

Jace made a sound of agreement. "Let me know when that happens. In the meantime, I'll keep looking for her."

Barrett assured him that he'd do the same, and when Della ended the call, he took out his own phone. However, before he could contact any of his deputies, the landline on the night-stand rang.

Considering that Barrett still didn't have his own cell phone, Della thought someone from his office might try to contact him this way, but with everything else going on, she moved closer to listen when he answered it. What Della heard sent her heart to her knees.

"I'm so sorry," the woman said.

Alice.

"Where are you?" Barrett demanded, and Della heard the emotional punch in his own voice, too.

Alice didn't respond, but there was some mumbling in the background. The woman wasn't alone. "I, uh, can't say," Alice finally muttered. There were more mumblings, but

Della couldn't make out the second voice. "You're supposed to come and rescue me. You and Della are supposed to come." Alice made a hoarse sob. "But please don't do it—"

And with that, the call cut off.

Della felt the fear slide through her. She hadn't needed any proof that whatever was happening was a setup to get to Barrett and her, but Alice had just confirmed it. That confirmation might have cost Alice big-time. Whoever had her probably was going to make her pay for blurting out that warning.

Cursing, Barrett hit redial, and Della heard the ringing. What she didn't hear though was anyone answering it, and with each ring, she could feel the stress rising inside her.

"The kidnapper won't kill her," Della assured him, and she tried to reassure herself, as well. But he or she would hurt her. In fact, the kidnapper might do all sorts of nasty things to get Barrett and her to come out into the open.

Where they'd almost certainly be killed.

When no one answered after nearly a minute, Barrett hung up and hit redial again. Like before, the ringing started. Then stopped. In fact, everything stopped, including the dial tone.

The line was dead.

That definitely didn't help Della tamp down her fear. Since there wasn't any bad weather to disrupt service, someone had almost certainly cut the line, and now they had no way to contact Alice. Of course, the kidnapper would figure out a way to contact Barrett and her. Della was sure of that.

Barrett still had his cell in his hand, and he hit the button to make a call. He frowned when he looked at the screen. "It's dead, too."

Della knew that wasn't a coincidence, and she held her breath while she checked her own phone. It was also dead.

"Someone's using a jammer," Barrett growled.

Della had heard about such things but didn't know a lot about them. However, what she did know was that the person using the jamming device had to be nearby. This wasn't something that would work from a long distance.

"You think someone set up a jammer here at your place?" Della asked.

Barrett didn't get a chance to answer before they heard something. Something that Della definitely didn't want to hear.

A woman screamed.

BARRETT FORCED HIMSELF to put aside the emotional punch he got from hearing that scream. Forced himself to think through what was happening. But one thing was for certain.

The scream had been close.

Damn close. In fact, he was pretty sure it had come from the vicinity of his own barn. Not good, since the barn was only yards from the house.

Barrett hurried to the window that faced the back of the house, and he peered out through the slats of the blinds. It was pitch-dark outside, not even a sliver of a moon thanks to some clouds, and the exterior lights were off. That in itself wasn't unusual. The lights got turned on only if he or one of his hands had work to do at night. But now Barrett needed those lights to try to figure out what was going on.

"No!" someone shouted.

Barrett still couldn't see anyone, but it helped him pinpoint the location of the person who'd shouted. Definitely the barn.

"That sounds like Alice," Della said, hurrying to the other side of the window to peer out.

Yeah, it did, though Barrett couldn't be positive. Still, it would make sense for the kidnapper to bring her here. It'd make it easier for him or her to try to get to them.

Barrett needed to make sure that didn't happen.

"Stay back from the window," he warned Della. "I want to check the security system."

Judging from the way Della sucked in her

breath, she hadn't realized that the alarm could be affected. It wasn't tied to the landline, but Barrett suspected that it, too, could be jammed.

Thankfully, Della stayed put, but she did ease back a little. However, he had no doubts that she'd continue to keep watch. She'd want to spot the woman who'd yelled and make sure that someone didn't try to get in through the back of the house.

Barrett cursed when he saw no lights on the security panel. It was definitely jammed. However, he did still have electricity and hopefully internet, too. He picked up the laptop, taking it back to the bedroom, and he used it to fire off emails to both his brothers. He filled them in on the situation and requested backup.

Backup with caution.

He'd emphasized that he didn't know what he was dealing with so they were to make a silent approach. Barrett had no idea if Jace, Leo or Daniel would even check their emails, but he hoped like the devil that they did.

"Do you see anything?" Barrett asked Della.

"No, but your barn door's closed." She paused, continued to peer through the blinds.

Yeah, he normally kept it closed at night. That didn't mean, though, that someone hadn't sneaked in there. And that led him to a thought that riled him to the core. Someone had slipped onto his property while he'd been asleep. That damn nap he'd taken could end up costing them.

"You're not going out there," Della said when she glanced at him adjusting his holster and checking his gun.

He'd debated it. Barrett wanted to know what was going on in that barn, and if Alice was in danger, he wanted to do his job and rescue her. But leaving the house meant one of two things. He either had to take Della with him or leave her inside and hope this wasn't a ploy to separate them so the kidnapper could have an easier time picking them off.

"I can give you backup," she reminded him, tapping her own holster that she'd put back on after they'd dressed.

She could. But the cost could be sky-high if anything went wrong. And with the kidnapper already nearby, plenty of things could go wrong.

"We'll wait a few minutes. I sent an email to Daniel and Leo, and if it goes through, I want to give them time to respond."

Della made a sound of agreement and went back to keeping watch. He knew the instant she'd seen something because of the change in her body language. She drew her gun, and Barrett hurried to the window, easing Della behind him.

"Someone opened the barn door just a fraction," Della relayed to him.

He could see that. But what he couldn't tell was if someone was still in the doorway. Without any lights on, everything was in the shadows.

"We'll have a better angle from the kitchen window," he said, considering that idea. Anyone who wanted to shoot them would have a better angle, too, since there were no blinds on that particular window and it was much larger than the one here in the bedroom. In fact, it spread out across nearly the entire kitchen wall.

"We can stay down," Della suggested.

True, but if they got in a position to see the barn door, then they were also in a position for the kidnapper to see them. Plus, Della and he wouldn't be able to shoot until they were certain Alice wouldn't be in the line of fire. Unless the kidnapper was an idiot, he or she would use Alice as a human shield.

But who was doing this?

Maybe another hired thug? Of course, it could be Rory. He was a PI after all, and if he was desperate enough, he might believe that killing Della and him would stall the investigation. Ditto for Curran. Heck, for Lorraine, too. In other words, Barrett couldn't eliminate any one of them.

"We'll stay down," Barrett verified, and he motioned for them to head to the kitchen.

Along the way, he checked the windows and doors to make sure no one was trying to break in. There were no signs of that, but he'd need to keep his ears honed for any unusual sounds.

Barrett stayed ahead of Della, and he paused in the living room to confirm that all was clear in the kitchen. It was. No one was lurking in there, ready to strike. And he'd been right about having a better angle on the barn. He saw it much better now, including the ajar door.

And the person standing inside.

He couldn't be positive, but he thought it was Alice.

Barrett didn't dare call out to her because he didn't want to give away their position in the house. However, he did move closer, motioning with his hand for Della to stay back. He went to the side of the window, trying to pick through the darkness.

That's when he saw the gun.

Someone had Alice in a choke hold and had a gun pointed at her head. Barrett had suspected things were this bad, but seeing it confirmed it. Too bad he couldn't tell if it was a man or a woman holding Alice, since the person was wearing long sleeves and gloves. Barrett also couldn't determine height since it appeared the person was hunched down, staying completely behind Alice.

He was so focused on watching the two figures that adrenaline and shock speared through him when the phone rang. Again, it was the landline, but he had an extension in the kitchen. Dropping down a little lower, he reached up and took the phone.

"Barrett," Alice said the moment he answered. He peered out the window again and saw the phone. Alice's captor had it gripped in the hand that he or she was using for the choke hold.

"Who has you?" Barrett asked.

Again, Alice didn't answer that, and now that his eyes had adjusted some to the darkness, he could see the grimace on her face. "I'm to tell you that Della and you need to come out. If not, we'll all die."

The kidnapper's plan was for them to all die no matter what. Barrett needed his own plan. One that would buy him some time with the hopes that backup would soon arrive.

"I'll come out," Barrett finally said. "But not Della. She took some pain meds for the gunshot wound, and they knocked her out."

He heard some whispers, saw Alice shake her head. Then, the choke hold tightened. The gun jammed even harder into her temple.

"You're to bring Della," Alice insisted. "Even if you have to carry her." She shook her head again, wincing, and Barrett also thought she was crying. "Don't come out here!" Alice shouted.

Just as the shot rang out.

DELLA'S BREATH STALLED in her lungs. Oh, God. Had Alice been shot?

She leaned out to get a better look, but Della didn't see anything. The two figures who'd been in the doorway of the barn weren't there. She doubted that was a good thing. Nor was the fact that she didn't hear any other shouts from Alice.

Barrett muttered some profanity, his gaze sweeping over the yard before it came back to her. "I'm going out the front door and will circle around back. I want you to stay put."

She was shaking her head before he even finished. "You need backup. Plus, it won't be any safer for me to be inside than it will to be with you. We need to check on Alice. If she's hurt…"

But Della didn't finish that. Couldn't. She couldn't let herself think the worst. Maybe the kidnapper had just fired a warning shot to keep Alice from trying to shout out to them. After all, whoever had taken her would need to keep her alive if for no other reason than to draw them out of the house.

And that's exactly what was happening.

They were cops, and a civilian was in grave danger. They had to do their jobs and stop it.

Of course, they also had to put aside the emotional part of this, since she doubted even Barrett could forget that it was his mother out there.

"I'll stay behind you," Della added, and she would have continued to try to persuade him if there hadn't been another sound.

Alice screamed again.

And there was a shot.

Both sounds had definitely come from inside the barn, and despite Della not wanting to think the worst, she believed that Alice might be fighting for her life.

Cursing, Barrett went to a closet in the adjoining living room and came back with a Kevlar vest. "I have just one, and you're wearing it," he insisted.

Della hated that he'd be going out there unprotected—while trying to shield her, no doubt—but this was the compromise that would prevent him from having to do this alone.

She set aside her gun to put on the vest. While she did that, Barrett took out two other guns from the cabinet over the fridge. "For backup," he said, tucking his in the waist of his jeans.

Della did the same to the gun he gave her, and as soon as she'd finished, they got moving. Good. She didn't want to wait another second to give Barrett time for second thoughts to settle in.

Barrett unlocked the front door, and he looked around the yard before he stepped out onto the porch. He made another sweep before he motioned for her to follow him. Della did, and she tried to settle her heartbeat drumming in her ears so that she'd be able to hear.

There were no other screams or shots, thank goodness. No sounds of footsteps or anyone approaching, either. Maybe Leo or Daniel would arrive soon to help, but if not, Barrett and she would have to make this work. He had the advantage, after all, of knowing every inch of his own property, and he used that advantage by ducking behind trees and shrubs as they made their way to the backyard.

Barrett stopped when they reached the back of the house and had another look around. They had a clear view of the barn now and the still open door, but there was no sign of Alice and her captor. Unfortunately, the captor might have a clear line of sight of Barrett and her when they crossed the yard to the barn. That's almost certainly why Della felt Barrett's hesitation, and she prayed he didn't turn around and go back.

The next sound stopped any thoughts of that.

There was some movement in the barn. But not ordinary movement. There seemed to be a struggle going on. A fight. One that Alice could be losing. Any of their suspects or a hired thug would be bigger and stronger than Alice. And that was likely why Barrett got them moving again.

Despite those sounds, Barrett didn't make a beeline for the barn. He went to the right, following a line of mountain laurels and a fence. Neither gave them much cover, but it was still better than being out in the open.

As they moved, Della kept watch behind them, hoping they wouldn't be ambushed. But they made it within ten feet of the barn before Barrett pulled to a quick stop. He whispered something, something that she didn't catch, but then she looked on the ground in the direction of where he was pointing.

What the heck?

It appeared to be a small black box, and there was a sound coming from it. Sharp clicks.

"It's a bomb like the one on the road," Barrett warned her. He hooked his arm around her waist and pulled her to the ground on the other side of one of the trees.

The explosion blasted through the air.

It was deafening, and it sent up a spray of debris that rained down on them. Della had no choice but to cover her head and hope that Barrett and she didn't get hurt. Barrett helped make sure that didn't happen—to her anyway. Keeping his gun ready, he crawled over her, shielding her with his body.

She wanted to curse him, to tell him not to risk his life like that, but she couldn't. Because he was thinking of the baby.

The moment the debris stopped falling, Barrett lifted his head, his gaze zooming around, but it didn't stay lifted for long. A shot came their way. The bullet smacked into the ground just a few feet away from them. Barrett covered her again just as a second shot smacked into the tree.

Della felt the raw mix of fear and adrenaline. Her breathing was too fast. Ditto for her pulse. But there was no way to settle her body when it was bracing for a fight. And screaming for her to get to Alice. If the kidnapper was firing at them, then that could mean Alice had been shot.

Or worse.

There were certainly no sounds of the woman now. Nor anything to indicate a struggle. Just the shots. Two more of them before everything went silent.

Della pulled in her breath, waiting and listening, but the seconds crawled by with no other shots. Barrett lifted his head again, glanced around.

"We'll crawl the rest of the way," he whispered. "Once we reach the barn, we'll run to the back and get in that way. Stay behind me, and if the shooter fires again, swear to me that you'll get down."

"I swear," Della said, and it was the truth. She couldn't risk being shot again. Not even while wearing the vest because it only covered her chest area. Even if the shot wasn't fatal, blood loss could cause her to lose the baby.

Barrett nodded. "Use the flashlight on your phone to check the ground," he instructed. "I don't want us stepping on a bomb."

Sweet heaven. She hadn't even considered that possibility, even though the last blast had only been minutes ago. Yes, it was possible that Alice's captor had left booby traps that could kill them.

Della continued to keep watch, but she used her phone to shine a light on the ground. Thankfully, it was mainly dirt that covered the back of the barn so a bomb would have been easy to spot. She didn't see anything. Didn't hear anything, either, which only caused her concerns to spike. It could mean that Alice was dead and that her captor was now lying in wait for Barrett and her.

"Stay low," Barrett whispered to her when they started to move again.

She did, and they hurried from the side to the rear double doors of the barn. Like the front, they were open. Not just ajar, though. Fully open. Almost as if it were an invitation for them to come in.

And be killed.

Barrett paused just outside those open doors, and he glanced around as if trying to figure out the safest way to approach this. He finally motioned for her to get down on the ground.

"All the way down," he muttered when Della crouched.

She wanted to insist that he get down, too, but now wasn't the time for an argument. The kidnapper could use the sound of their voices to pinpoint their location. If so, shots could easily go through the barn walls.

Della went belly down on the ground and levered up her torso in case she had to shoot. Barrett stooped, hunkering down, but he also kept his gun aimed and ready.

"Alice?" he called out, his voice shattering the silence.

Della steeled herself up for a gunshot. One that hopefully wouldn't hit them because of their positions.

But nothing.

"Alice?" Barrett repeated, louder this time.

Still nothing. And that's when Della saw something in the dirt. Footprints. They looked recent, and they were leading away from the barn and toward a wooded area to the left of the pasture.

"Hell," Barrett growled. "The kidnapper's getting away."

Chapter Seventeen

Barrett fired glances all around him. He listened, too, but he couldn't see any signs of Alice or the person who'd taken her. And unfortunately, those footprints led into some thick clusters of trees. Beyond that, there was a ranch trail.

Which would make for an easy escape route.

Before Barrett took off in that direction, though, he peered around the edge of the barn door and looked inside. It was too dark so he risked turning on the lights. Part of him half expected to see Alice, maybe sprawled out on the floor. But there was no sign of her. However, there were signs of a struggle.

Hay bales had been toppled over, and the loose hay on the ground had been strewn around. The pitchfork that should have been on the hook mounted on the wall had been tossed in front of one of the stalls. It was possible Alice had tried to use it against her captor during the struggle that Barrett had heard.

"No blood," Della said, and that's when he realized she'd crawled in behind him. She got to her feet, moving clear of the open door, and she looked around.

Yeah, no blood was a good thing. It meant Alice was still alive, but she might not stay that way for long.

"Why would the kidnapper have left with Alice?" Della muttered, but it sounded as if she was talking to herself.

"Maybe he or she thought it was too risky to stay put," Barrett suggested. "Or maybe the kidnapper's just regrouping to make another go at us."

Della didn't have a chance to give her opinion on that because they heard a sound. Not a gunshot. But another shout. And Barrett was betting it had come from Alice.

"No!" Her voice echoed through the woods.

Doing another quick check of the grounds, Barrett stepped outside and pinpointed where the sound had come from. Definitely in the direction of the ranch trail. It was possible the kidnapper had parked a vehicle there and was now trying to move Alice.

He had a short debate with himself about what to do. Della and he could hurry back to the front of the house and get the cruiser, but it'd take him a while to get to that trail since he'd have to go back up the road. Judging from Alice's scream, she didn't have that kind of time.

"Stay behind me," Barrett reminded Della again.

He took off, not running exactly because he didn't want to kick up the pace too much and force Della to keep up with him. He stayed at a light jog, keeping watch, listening.

There was another shouted, "No," and he was pretty sure there was a struggle going on. Whatever was happening, Alice seemed to be fighting it. Good. The fact that she was alive and still able to try to defend herself might mean that Della and he could get to her in time.

Barrett just hoped the cost wouldn't be too high.

After all, each step they took put them closer to a would-be killer. One that had targeted Della.

"Don't shoot," someone whispered, causing Barrett and Della to come to a quick halt.

Barrett caught onto Della, yanking her behind a tree with him, and he glanced around, looking for the person who'd spoken.

"Don't shoot," the man repeated.

Judging from Della's groan, she recognized the voice. So did Barrett, and it didn't make him lower his guard.

Because it was Rory.

Hell. Was he the one who'd kidnapped Alice? If so, Alice wasn't making any noise now, and Barrett didn't hear anyone moving around. As close as Rory was, he would have definitely heard something.

"Come out with your hands up," Barrett warned him, and he tried to keep his voice as low as possible. If Rory wasn't the kidnapper, then Barrett didn't want Alice's real captor hearing any of this.

"I want to help you," Rory answered. He was whispering as well, and each word came out shaky and hoarse.

"You can help by doing what I just told you. Come out and keep your hands where I can see them."

Behind him, Barrett could feel Della trembling. Could feel her breath gusting. But she also had her gun aimed, ready to take out the man if he was a threat.

Barrett certainly hadn't expected Rory to just surrender. And that's why he was shocked when the man did. Rory stepped out from behind a large oak. He still had his gun gripped in his hand, but he'd lifted his arms over his head.

"Drop your gun," Barrett ordered. "Kick it toward me."

"I need to keep it," Rory argued. "Someone has your mother, and she needs our help."

Considering that Rory had killed his own sister, obstructed justice and then gone on the run, Barrett didn't have a lot of faith in any help the man could give them. Still, Rory was right. Someone did have Alice.

Maybe Rory.

"Drop your gun now," Barrett ordered, and he made sure Rory knew he meant business.

Rory swallowed hard, tossed down his gun and, as instructed, kicked it toward Barrett. He then put his hands back up in the air.

"Did you kidnap Alice?" Barrett came out and asked.

Rory's eyes widened. "No. Of course, not."

"Then, what the hell are you doing out here?"

"I came to talk to you. To try to explain that I'm not responsible for the attacks." His voice broke. "I needed your help."

Maybe, but something about this didn't mesh. "Where's your car?" Barrett demanded.

Rory tipped his head in the direction of the road. "I stopped and parked when I saw Della and you run out of the house and toward the barn. I figured something was wrong."

Barrett wanted to laugh. Yeah, something was definitely wrong. And Rory might be a big part of that.

"I slipped into the trees so I could see what was happening," Rory went on. "I heard someone running. Maybe fighting. Not Della and you. You were still by the barn. This was someone else, and when I went deeper into the woods, I caught a glimpse of your mother."

Everything inside Barrett went still. "If you saw my mother, then you also saw the person who has her."

Rory nodded. "But I couldn't make out who it was. The person was wearing a ski mask or something." Another pause. "He had a gun to your mother's head."

"He?" Della and Barrett questioned in unison.

Rory opened his mouth, closed it and obviously reconsidered. "Maybe it was a man. Like I said, I only got a glimpse."

Too bad that brief look hadn't told them more than they already knew. Someone had Alice. And now they had the added problem of what to do with Rory. Barrett had no intention of trusting the man. For all he knew, Rory had Alice stashed somewhere and was pretending to be an innocent bystander to this mess.

But the next sound Barrett heard had him rethinking that.

A gunshot.

It hadn't been fired directly at them, but he

thought the shooter was likely by that ranch trail that was still a good fifty yards away.

"Turn around," he told Rory. Barrett took out a pair of plastic cuffs, whirled Rory around when he didn't listen and restrained the man.

"I can help you," Rory protested.

But he was talking to himself. Barrett scooped up Rory's gun, tucking it in the back waist of his jeans.

"Let's go," he told Della. "You stay put," he added to Rory.

Whether the man would do that was anyone's guess, but Barrett didn't have time to deal with that now. At least Rory wouldn't be able to come up from behind and shoot them. Not with his hands cuffed behind him. He wouldn't be able to put up much of a fight, either.

Just as they'd done when they started their run, Della stayed behind Barrett, and when he glanced over his shoulder, he saw that she was keeping watch, as well. He kept them moving fast, heading toward the sound of that last gunshot. Even though it wasn't that far, it seemed to take a lifetime or two, and with each step, he was reminded of the danger that was no doubt waiting for them.

Barrett stopped when they were only a couple of yards away, and he pulled down one of the low-hanging tree branches so he could try to spot any vehicle.

He did.

There was a black car parked on the trail. The headlights were off, but the engine was running, and the back passenger's side door was open. The light from the car's interior speared through the darkness, allowing Barrett to see.

Alice was on the ground, in a fight with someone dressed all in black. Someone with a gun.

And that someone fired a shot at Alice.

"STOP!" DELLA SHOUTED though she wasn't sure how she'd managed to speak. What she saw had caused her throat muscles to clamp tight.

Della's cop training kicked in, and she took aim at the person who'd fired that shot. But she couldn't shoot back. She didn't have a safe shot, not with Alice in the line of fire. And not with the kidnapper dragging Alice by her hair into the back seat of the vehicle. Alice had stopped struggling, and there was fresh blood on her face, but she seemed to be alive.

Barrett's training must have kicked in, too, because he muscled Della back behind the meager cover of the tree. He joined her there, leaning out so he could see the car. Della did the same from the other side, but she knew Barrett would want her on the ground if the shooter pulled the trigger again.

"Has Alice been shot?" Della muttered, figuring that Barrett wouldn't hear her.

Even if he had, he likely wouldn't have known the answer. The kidnapper shut the door, cutting off the light and making it impossible for them to see inside the vehicle. Della certainly hadn't been able to tell if the person who had Alice was a man or a woman.

"If he or she tries to drive out of here, I'll shoot out the tires," Barrett told her. "That might not stop the car, but it'll slow it down."

True, and then they could hopefully go in pursuit. It wouldn't be easy on foot, but the driver wouldn't have an easier time of it, either. There was no way to turn around on this part of the trail. It wasn't nearly wide enough for that, and trees lined both sides. The driver would have to go in Reverse in the dark.

"We need to talk," Barrett shouted out. "I understand it's me you want. If so, let Alice go."

Nothing.

Well, nothing from the car anyway. But there was a rustling sound behind them that had both Della and Barrett pivoting in that direction.

"It's me," someone said. *Daniel.* "I got your email."

The relief rushed through Della. They had

backup. Something they might need before this was over.

Daniel snaked his way through the trees and took cover behind the one that was directly across from them. "Other than Alice, any idea who's inside?" he asked.

"No," Barrett answered. "But I think we're about to find out," he amended when the back window lowered.

Della saw Alice, and yes, the woman was definitely bleeding. There was a thick streak of it making its way down the side of her face. She looked dazed, too, maybe because of another head injury, or it was possible the kidnapper had managed to drug her.

The kidnapper was no longer next to Alice but was instead in the front seat, behind the steering wheel. A gloved hand was extended over the seat, and the gun was once again pointed at Alice's head. Della heard the driver mutter something. Then, Alice groaned and nodded.

"You need to back off," Alice told them, no doubt repeating the instructions she'd just been given. Her words were slurred. "If you don't, I'll die. We'll all die."

A moment later, the car engine started. And Barrett took aim at the tires.

"Don't," Alice said. Again, it was a repeat of what had come from the driver.

Della wished she could hear the kidnapper's actual voice, and then they'd know better what they were dealing with. It might be easier to negotiate if they knew the person's identity.

"I won't shoot out the tires if you don't try to drive off," Barrett countered. "You obviously came here to talk. So talk, and tell me what the hell you want."

There was another sound behind them, causing Barrett, Daniel and Della to pivot in that direction. It was Leo, and he had latched on to Rory's arm.

"Any chance this clown will be able to help with the negotiations?" Leo asked. He'd obviously heard at least the last bits of conversation.

Rory shook his head. "I don't know who's doing this."

Maybe. But Della wasn't going to buy that until she had some proof. And that's why she tested the waters. "We have Rory Silva," she called out.

More mutterings came from the driver. "So what?" Alice repeated.

That could indeed mean he'd had no part in this, or the kidnapper could be covering for him. Leo must have felt the same way because he pushed Rory into a sitting position on the ground.

"Stay put," Leo warned him.

"Well?" Barrett shouted to the driver. "Since you're not driving off, I expect you to tell me what you want."

There was a short silence, followed by whispered instructions from the kidnapper. Instructions that caused Alice to turn and look at the person. She shook her head as if trying to come out of her dazed state.

"I can't do that," Alice insisted. She was speaking not to them but to her captor. "You'll just have to kill me."

"What does the kidnapper want you to do?" Barrett demanded.

Alice looked at him. "To trade me for you. I won't do that." Alice's voice was still shaky, but there was plenty of determination in her tone and expression before she turned back to the driver. "None of this will help you. It's too late. You need to give yourself up."

It sounded as if Alice knew the identity of her captor. Barrett must have thought so, too, because he called out again. "Who kidnapped you, Alice? Who's doing this?"

The words had no sooner left Barrett's mouth than the driver hit the accelerator, and the black car began to speed away in Reverse. True to his word, Barrett shot at the tires. So did Leo and Daniel, and they hit the two on the side of the vehicle that was facing them. They also took off, running to catch up with the kidnapper.

The shot-out tires definitely didn't stop the car, but obviously the driver was having trouble staying on the narrow trail because he or she clipped a tree with the rear bumper. There was the sound of metal scraping against wood and some splinters flew, but the driver continued.

So did all four cops.

They darted through the trees, using them for cover, while continuing to shoot into the car. The engine this time. They couldn't risk firing into the windshield because Alice could be hit.

One of the bullets must have hit the radiator because steam started to spew from the car. It was enough of a distraction, and it caused the driver to hit another tree. Harder this time, and it ripped off the bumper. It also slowed down the vehicle enough for Barrett to catch up.

"No!" Alice shouted, and she turned in the seat and tried to hit the driver. It wasn't enough to stop the kidnapper from pulling the trigger.

The shot blasted through the driver's window, shattering the glass and sending it spewing.

Barrett ducked and Della prayed it was in time and he hadn't been hit. She couldn't see any blood on him. However, she did see something that sent her heart leaping to her throat.

Lorraine.

The woman was behind the wheel of the car. Her face was tight with rage and desperation.

And she fired another shot at Barrett.

WITH ALL HELL breaking loose, Barrett dived to the ground, and he pulled Della down with him. He tried to keep her behind him, as much out of harm's way as he could manage, but there wasn't any safe place for her.

Not with Lorraine firing shots at them.

Worse, she was maybe shooting at Alice, too, and unlike them, Alice could get hit at point-blank range. Still, he could hear his mother shouting. Could hear the struggle going on in the car.

And Barrett wanted to know why this was happening.

He hoped he got the chance to question Lorraine about it, but he figured this had to go back to Casto. If Lorraine had hired LeBeau and the others to rough up Casto and Alice and then things had gotten out of hand, it could have led to murder. It might lead to another one, too, if he didn't do something fast.

"Wait here with Della," Barrett told Daniel.

Della wouldn't like that order, but there was a chance that Lorraine wasn't doing this alone. She could have hired other thugs to help her do whatever it was she was trying to do. Maybe kill anyone involved in the investigation so that she wouldn't be brought to justice?

If that was her motive, then Barrett needed to make sure she failed.

Another shot blasted through the air, and he tried not to think of Lorraine putting Della and therefore the baby in danger. Barrett shut all of that out and focused on getting to the car.

At least the vehicle was no longer moving, thanks to Lorraine. She'd bashed it into a tree, and the now flat tires had gotten wedged in the shallow ditch. Lorraine might still be able to get the car going, but that wasn't going to happen while she was still fighting Alice.

And she was fighting her.

Alice used her tied up hands like a club and swiped at Lorraine, but Lorraine ducked and bashed her gun against Alice's head. Alice groaned in pain and slumped against the seat. She wasn't unconscious, but Alice was clearly dazed. Too bad because as long as Lorraine was focused on Alice, she wouldn't have seen Barrett coming at her.

But she did see him.

Lorraine climbed over the seat, positioning herself behind Alice, and when the woman took aim at him from over Alice's shoulder, Barrett had no choice but to drop to the ground and roll to the side and take cover behind the tree that Lorraine's car had hit.

"I'll kill her. So help me God, I will," Lorraine shouted.

She sounded as if she'd totally lost it. Looked it, too. Obviously, she hadn't counted on things getting this messed up. Maybe she'd thought she could use Alice to draw out Della and him, kill them, and then her life would go back to normal.

Fat chance of that.

Lorraine might get off more shots, but eventually she'd have to reload, and that's when Barrett could charge at her. Or take his own shot. He couldn't do that now, though. Not with Alice directly in front of Lorraine.

"Stay back!" Lorraine shouted when Leo moved closer. "I'm leaving with Alice, and the only way to keep her alive is to put down your guns so I can get out of here."

For Lorraine to drive, she'd have to climb back over the seat. And while doing that, she'd lose her human shield. When she realized that, Barrett was concerned Lorraine might turn this into a suicide mission, along with taking out as many of them as she could.

"How the heck did you convince Alice that you'd taken me hostage?" Barrett asked. He didn't especially care, but he wanted to keep Lorraine focused on his voice. Wanted to keep her talking. That way, maybe Leo could get in a position to take out the woman.

"I recorded our conversations at the sheriff's office," Lorraine admitted. She kept the gun propped on Alice's shoulder, pointed in Barrett's direction, but she could easily turn it and shoot Alice in the head. "Then, I spliced together sentences using an audio editor app I bought."

Lorraine sounded smug about that accomplishment. Smug and on the verge of losing it. He could see the woman's hand shaking. And bleeding. Barrett noticed that she, too, had a head injury.

From the corner of his eye, he also saw Leo. He was belly down, crawling over the ditch and onto the trail. His plan was no doubt to get to the other side of the car so he could come at Lorraine from behind.

"You obviously need medical attention. How'd you get hurt?" Barrett asked Lorraine. Again, not because he cared, but he needed the sound of his voice to cover up Leo's movement.

"The bitch hit me with a pitchfork," Lorraine spat out, and that must have caused a surge of anger because she bashed her gun against Alice's head again. "She fought like a wildcat to save her *little boy*." Lorraine's voice dripped with a combination of venom and sarcasm on the last two words.

But Barrett wasn't feeling either of those things. It tightened his gut to know that Alice had tried to protect him. And it had put her in the hands of this lunatic.

"You jammed my phone," Barrett called out to Lorraine. "You're also the one who hired Ezell."

He needed to give Leo more time, along with maybe distracting Lorraine so that she wouldn't hit Alice again. Alice was barely conscious now, and she was moaning in pain. It was possible that Lorraine had fractured Alice's skull.

"Of course, I did," Lorraine snapped. "Using the jammer was something that Harris LeBeau taught me way back when. That and where to buy explosives for the bomb I set on the road. I couldn't have you calling for your brothers so I used a jammer," Lorraine snapped. "For all the good it did. You obviously got word to them somehow."

Yeah, he had, and Lorraine was about to come face-to-face with the result of Leo getting the "word." Barrett saw Leo peer into the window behind Lorraine. If his brother was fast enough, Leo could throw open the door, latch on to Lorraine and drag her out of the car before the woman could get off another shot. Especially a shot that could be fatal.

But that didn't happen.

Lorraine must have heard or sensed something because she whirled in Leo's direction, and the woman turned her gun toward him.

"Watch out!" Della shouted, both Daniel and her moving closer.

Barrett moved, too. So did Alice. His mother hit the gun just as Lorraine fired.

The bullet slammed into Alice.

The blood splattered all over Lorraine, all over the car. Barrett didn't want to think about Alice being dead. He needed to do his job and put an end to the danger.

Barrett pushed forward, moving ahead of Della and Daniel. Since Lorraine still had hold of the gun, he charged at her before she could take aim at him.

But she didn't.

With Leo gripped onto her shoulders, Lorraine still managed to turn the gun on herself.

And she pulled the trigger.

Chapter Eighteen

It was chaos. A different kind of chaos than there'd been just minutes earlier when Barrett, his brothers and Della had been trying to stop Lorraine. Lorraine had ended her life but had left plenty of mess to clean up.

The ambulance siren wailed as it came to a stop on the ranch trail, and the EMTs sprang into action. Good. Because Alice needed medical attention ASAP.

Leo had moved Lorraine's lifeless body off Alice, and both Della and he were trying to slow Alice's bleeding from the gunshot wound.

Not to her head, thank God.

That'd been where Lorraine had intended the bullet to go, but the shot instead had slammed into the top of Alice's shoulder. She was losing a lot of blood, and it didn't help that she had the other injuries Lorraine had given her during their struggle. She was conscious—that was something at least—but Barrett could tell from her moans that she was in a lot of pain.

It didn't matter that Alice and he hadn't had the best of relationships. He still hated to see her suffer. Especially because of him. Alice had hit Lorraine's gun to stop him from being shot.

His mother had literally taken a bullet meant for him.

No way to dismiss that. No way that it couldn't matter. It did. And Barrett felt a barrier or two lower between Alice and him.

Della climbed out of the back seat of Lorraine's car so the EMTs could have access to Alice. Barrett wasn't far, only a few yards away, and he went to Della not only to try to steady her. To steady himself, too. He pulled Della into his arms and held on. She gave a weary sigh and melted against him.

"You should check out Della, too," Alice insisted. Her words were a little slurred, but that came through clear enough to give Barrett another jolt of fear.

"Are you okay?" he asked, moving Della back so he could look at her. "Were you hit?"

"No," Della answered. "I'm all right." She checked him over, too, no doubt to make sure the same was true for him. Lorraine had fired a lot of shots, and any one of them could have hit his brothers, Della or him.

"The baby," Alice added, and her eyelids fluttered down. "I heard Della and you talking about it. Della needs to be checked because of the baby."

So, that's how Alice had found out. And after one look at Leo and Daniel, Barrett realized that they now knew, too.

"Yeah," Barrett confirmed. "Della's pregnant with my baby." He hadn't meant that to have the edge of a threat, but he didn't want his brothers giving him any grief.

They didn't.

Leo and Daniel exchanged looks of mutual surprise, and then grins. "Figured you and Della had gotten back together," Leo added. "Didn't know you were *this* back together."

Barrett nearly blurted out that the pregnancy wasn't planned, but that might seem as if he was somehow dismissing it.

He wasn't.

Barrett wasn't sure when it had happened, but this baby had moved to the top of his list of priorities. The baby, along with Della, of course.

"So, what will you do about it?" Leo asked, and he had enough of a grin to make Barrett scowl at him.

"I'll get back to you on that," Barrett grumbled. Because, heck, he wasn't the one in the driver's seat here. The real question was—what was Della going to do about it? Was she going to let him be a big part of her and the baby's life?

"She's lost some blood," one of the medics said, getting Barrett's attention. "We've got her stabilized for now but we need to take her to the hospital."

The other medic hurried back to the ambulance to bring out a gurney. The two immediately started to move Alice onto it. Despite all the jostling around, Alice still managed to make eye contact with him.

"I'm so sorry about all of this," Alice told him. "If I hadn't been so stupid, none of this would have happened."

Barrett shook his head. He could definitely give her an out on this. "Lorraine was desperate. If she hadn't used you, she would have found a way to try to get to us."

And it likely hadn't helped Alice's state of mind to believe that a pregnant Della was in danger. Alice hadn't exactly been mother of the year, but it was obvious that she still had some maternal feelings for her offspring.

"We'll be at the hospital soon," Della assured Alice as the EMTs put the woman into the ambulance.

Alice managed a nod. "You can have yourself checked out, too."

That wasn't a bad idea, and maybe Della

wouldn't argue with him about it. He was betting her nerves were as raw as his, and a little reassurance from the doctor could help.

"I'll deal with him," Leo said, hauling Rory to his feet. "My cruiser's parked at your house."

Barrett certainly hadn't forgotten about Francine's brother, but it was the beginning of some "chaos" for Rory, too. Leo would book him on an assortment of charges stemming from Francine's death. But for now, Barrett had one question for the man.

"Did you have anything to do with what Lorraine did tonight?" Barrett demanded.

"No." Rory said it with plenty of conviction, too. "Like I said, I just came over to talk, and I saw Alice getting dragged away. I didn't even know it was Lorraine until after we got out here and she started talking."

Barrett kept a hard stare on the man long enough to see if it would make him squirm from any lies he'd told. But there wasn't any squirming. Maybe Rory truly hadn't had anything to do with Lorraine. Even so, the man would get jail time for the other charges.

So would Curran.

It was ironic that Lorraine had been able to give them the proof that would finally put Curran behind bars. If Lorraine weren't already dead, Curran likely would have wanted to get back at her for that.

"I can wait here for the medical examiner and the crime scene unit," Daniel said as the ambulance began to back out down the trail.

Barrett nodded, thankful for the offer. He really wanted to get Della to the hospital. Apparently, Leo was in a hurry, too, because he headed back through the woods with Rory in tow.

Daniel gave another glance at the ambulance before he turned back to Barrett. "Are you all right about being with Alice at the hospital?"

It was as simple a question as it seemed. A lot of years and bad blood had gone into their feelings for their mother.

Barrett nodded. "I just don't want to hang on to the bad stuff any longer."

Seemingly amused, Daniel flexed his eyebrows when he glanced at Della. "Obviously, this baby and you have had an effect on him."

Della smiled when Daniel did. "Are you all right with being an uncle again?" she asked.

"You bet," Daniel assured her. He leaned over and brushed a kiss on Della's cheek. "Now, put Barrett out of his misery and kiss him. He looks like he's ready to implode or something."

Barrett hoped to hell that wasn't how he

looked. He was trying his best to level out so that Della would do the same.

"Come on," Barrett said, slipping his arm around Della to get her moving. It wasn't a long walk back to his house, but they'd have to make their way through the woods again.

Della took a few steps but then stopped. She leaned in and kissed him. At first Barrett thought that maybe she did that because Daniel had brought it up. But when her mouth lingered on his, and she deepened the kiss, Barrett figured out that his brother had had no part in this.

"Better?" Della asked, easing back from him. She ran her tongue over her bottom lip, causing his body to clench. Considering everything they'd just gone through, it was an unexpected reaction.

But definitely a welcome one.

That's why Barrett pulled her back to him and kissed her. He needed to feel the familiar heat. Needed to be reminded that they'd come out of this alive.

He let the kiss linger another moment, until the heat really kicked in and let him know that when it came to Della and him, there was a fine line between a kiss and full-blown foreplay.

He was quickly crossing that line.

That's why Barrett got her walking again, but there was no need for the crazy pace they'd needed to get to Alice in time. And speaking of Alice, that was another reason for him not to go back in for another kiss. If Della and he kept it up, they wouldn't get to the hospital anytime soon.

"How much of a hassle are you going to give me about being examined by the doctor?" he asked.

"None," she readily answered. "I'm positive the doctor won't find anything wrong, but it won't hurt."

No, and it would make them both rest easier. Well, when they actually got rest, that is. Barrett was hoping it wouldn't be too long before that happened. While he was hoping, he added the hope that Alice's injuries wouldn't be that serious, and that way he could get Della off her feet. And that led him to his next question.

"Are you going to give me any hassle about staying at my place for a while?" he asked.

She stopped, looked up at him. "None."

Barrett smiled. He liked the way this conversation was going. "Good. Because I want you in my bed tonight."

Della smiled, too. Obviously, she hadn't gotten the memo on the fine line between kissing/ foreplay because the next kiss she gave him was long, hard and deep. Just the way he liked his kisses from Della. When she pulled back this time, he expected to see the glaze of lust—and it was there. But there was something else.

"I know the timing is off, but tell me how you feel about this baby," she said.

Barrett didn't even have to think about it. "I love him or her." That was the easy part. It was automatic, and the love went bone-deep. The hard part came, though, as well. "The kid deserves better than me for a father."

Della shook her head, smiled a little and got them walking away. "There's no one better than you. I know it. Soon, this baby will know it, too."

Mercy, she had a lot of trust in him, and for some reason, it made Barrett feel as if he could trust himself. He'd been a kid when he'd tried to help his grandfather raise Daniel and Leo. He wasn't one now. And the stakes were sky-high, so he'd have to do whatever it took to love and raise this baby.

Whatever it took to have Della, as well.

Because he was in love with her.

That hit him like a meaty fist and robbed him of some of his breath. He was in love with Della.

When the heck had that happened?

Maybe it'd been when he had come so close to losing her. Of course, it was possible that the love for her had always been there, but he'd just finally got around to admitting it.

Barrett stopped, turning her so he could give her another kiss. He was hoping the heat would work some magic because he needed all the help he could get. When he pulled back, she was a little breathless and still had a trace of a smile on her incredible mouth.

"How much of a hassle are you going to give me if I tell you I'm in love with you?" he asked.

Her smile widened. "None. Because I'm in love with you."

Della laughed—probably because he looked dumbfounded that it hadn't taken any coaxing. Not that he wanted coaxing. He wanted her "none" and everything that went along with it.

Still chuckling, Della slid her arm back around him. "How much of a hassle will you give me if I ask you to marry me?" she said.

Now, this was easy. So was the kiss Barrett gave her before he answered, "None."

* * * * *

Look for Safeguarding the Surrogate,
the next book in USA TODAY
bestselling author
Delores Fossen's Mercy Ridge
Lawmen series,
coming in July 2021!

Get 4 FREE REWARDS!

We'll send you 2 FREE Books plus 2 FREE Mystery Gifts.

FREE Value Over $20

Both the **Romance** and **Suspense** collections feature compelling novels written by many of today's bestselling authors.